MORE
GLIMPSES

The Second Collection of Short Stories

by

Hugh W. Roberts

Mumbleton Pier Publishing

First published March 2019
by Mumbleton Pier Publishing.

Cover design by George Grey (royalstondesign.com) All rights reserved.
Book design: David Cronin.

For more information about the author and upcoming books online,
please visit www.hughsviewsandnews.com

Contents

Dedication

To Holly, Lenny, and Isabella Grace.
Taking the family into the future.

Acknowledgments

Many of the stories in this book were made up from ideas or writing prompts from the blogging community. My thanks go to all the writers and bloggers who host writing challenges every week, especially to Charli Mills at the Carrot Ranch – https://carrotranch.com/ – and Sue Vincent at Sue Vincent's Daily Echo – https://scvincent.com/ – who publish a different writing challenge every week. I may not participate in these challenges every week, but I always thoroughly enjoy them, as well as reading the stories the challenges produce.

I'd also like to thank everyone who leaves a comment on my blog posts, which have gone on to spark off an idea for a story. These include Ali Isaac, for a comment that resulted in the story Fast Forward and to Colleen Chesebro, for a comment that resulted in the story Fairies At The Bottom Of The Garden. I would also like to thank the DJ, Sara Cox, for providing me with the idea for the story 'The Hole' after hearing her promoting her new show on the radio.

As I continue to learn about the art of writing, neither this book (nor my first book, Glimpses) would have been possible without all the support and encouragement from the writing community over at WordPress. My thanks to all the authors, writers, and bloggers who publish free writing and publishing tips and to everyone who has offered to promote this book for me.

Finally, my thanks to my editor, Esther Chilton, who helps me develop my stories, to George Grey for designing yet another excellent book cover, and to David Cronin for doing a wonderful job with formatting the book.

About This Book

'More Glimpses' was written because of the success of my first collection of short stories, Glimpses. The appetite my readers had for stories that come with an unexpected ending spurred me on in writing this new collection. It's taken almost two years to put together, but that's because I wanted all the stories in it to appeal to those who asked for more. I didn't want to rush into publishing a new collection, even though I was hoping to get a second collection published by the end of 2017.

This time, many of the stories have never been published before, even though the desire to publish them on my blog tormented me every time I finished a story. I wanted this collection to have lots of short stories that have never been read before. I've also included more drama and comedy related stories, something I never dreamt I would write, simply because I always thought stories under those genres could never come with shocking twists. How wrong I was! However, that's for you, the reader, to decide.

I've put together a good mixture of stories, from science-fiction to the paranormal, from horror to romantic comedy; all in all, there's something, I hope, for everyone.

Finally, I have used my dyslexia to help me, rather than hinder me, with my creation and writing of these stories. I have heard it said that those with the condition have rather remarkable creative minds. I'd love to know what you think. You can find my contact details at the back of this book.

About the Stories

The Whistle
Genre: Drama

Set in war-torn France in 1918, a soldier reflects on his life while he waits for the sound of the whistle, a sound that not only may signal the oncoming end of his life but reveal a secret the world can never ever find out.

Upside-Down and Inside-Out
Genre: Fantasy

Prudence Pebblebottom doesn't believe her mother has agoraphobia and ends up giving her a heart attack when forcing her to go outside. As the only beneficiary of her mother's will, Prudence is in for a nasty surprise when her world is literally turned upside-down.

Baby Talk
Genre: Comedy

A conversation a seven-month-old baby overhears its mother having with a shop assistant, has it screaming the place down. However, there are worthy reasons for the baby wanting to make a quick escape from the store.

The Bag Lady
Genre: Science Fiction

On a time travelling mission to the year 1999, three elderly ladies from the year 1961 find themselves in grave danger when pursued by another time traveller. Can they escape and get back to 1961 with the item the other time traveller so desperately wants to get off them?

The Tunnel
Genre: Action/Adventure

Filled with hazards and situations that can kill, a life-changing prize awaits all who enter the tunnel, with whoever gets to the prize first having the greater chance of coming out alive. However, be quick to find it as the prize doesn't wait around for long.

Tiny People
Genre: Horror

All over the world, mobile phones have been catching fire. Max Cumberland thinks he has the answer as to why it's happening. Convincing the mobile phone manufacturers, however, is going to be hard work.

Murder in Evershot
Genre: Murder/Mystery

Set in the sleepy, English village of Evershot, John, Toby, Austin, and Hugh find themselves in grave danger when several murders take place. Can they find a well-known detective, who lives in the village, and ask for her help in solving the murders before the murderer finds them?

Floral Hall
Genre: Paranormal

Boarded up and unused for many years, Floral Hall was once a place full of music, love, and laughter. Tim, a young boy out for a walk with his mother and grandmother, thinks he can hear music and laughter coming from the old building. Is Floral Hall about to reveal its secrets?

The Right Choice
Genre: Science Fiction

With the choice of facing the killer bees or the old ruins for a one-million-pounds prize, two gameshow contestants have only twenty seconds to make the right choice. Will they make the right one?

Knock, Knock
Genre: Horror

A prankster plays 'knock, knock' on the front door of a house. Inside, a 'home-alone' young girl, Angela, and her younger sister are terrified when the prankster threatens to kill them. When Angela finally gets the courage to open the door, she discovers it's not only whoever was knocking at the door that has disappeared.

Fast Forward
Genre: Science Fiction

Fascinated by the hidden feature on his new smartwatch, Brad gets the chance to time travel. As he travels forward, he doesn't like all that he witnesses and decides that it is time to travel back to the present. However, he's forgotten one vital piece of information. Can he get back safely before it's too late?

The Jump
Genre: Horror

Jane has murder on her mind and gives her husband, who suffers from vertigo, a parachute jump for his 50th birthday. Jumping out of the plane first, she gets a shock when landing on her island paradise where she thinks her lover is waiting for her. What awaits Jane is a nightmare beyond imagination.

Big Brother
Genre: Science Fiction

Have you ever wondered why files and photographs suddenly go missing from your computer, tablet or phone? Big Brother has the answer.

Tap
Genre: Horror

At a car boot sale, two teenagers do the unthinkable and steal items off the stall belonging to a blind man. What follows will not only change their lives but will haunt them forever.

Harvest Festival

Genre: Science Fiction

Harvest festival – a time of celebration and thanks for what has been provided to get us all through the upcoming long, hard winter. It should never be the time of nightmares, should it?

The Hole

Genre: Horror

Why do the same two dogs visit the garden of Elizabeth Jones every day and sniff at the same area? Wanting to know the answer, Elizabeth digs a hole at the spot where the dogs sniff. Will she find anything?

Easter Bunny Cake

Genre: Horror

For centuries, the Easter Bunny has been trying to find a way to punish naughty humans. Is simply not leaving them a chocolate egg the only answer?

Double Eighteen

Genre: Rom Com

Quentin has a brand-new girlfriend, Maureen, and he's determined to win them a romantic weekend for two in Paris, at the local pub's darts competition. On the evening of the match, something terrible happens, giving many of the regulars a shock.

The Man In The Television

Genre: Horror

Unaware of what is in the room with them, a family watching a popular Saturday evening television show have no idea what is really happening in front of them. Have you seen the man in the television?

Dream Catcher

Genre: Horror

How often are we told to follow our dreams? And what happens if we actually catch one? Does it give our dream a better chance of coming true? One man, who actually caught a dream, reveals all.

One-Hundred
Genre: Science-Fiction

If something wanted to kill off most of humanity, what would be the most unlikely weapon it could use? And are you one of the humans it wants to kill?

When The Tide Turns
Genre: Horror

On a day out, three young men discover a beautiful, deserted beach. However, despite a warning from an old man not to venture onto the sand, they take no notice, resulting in horrifying consequences for all of them.

Honeymoon
Genre: Rom-Com

Having just got married, it's the night of the honeymoon for Sylvia and Marty. Marty is eager to get things started, but Sylvia has something else on her mind.

The Truth About Waiting Rooms
Genre: Horror

Like or loath them, waiting rooms are everywhere, and we all find ourselves in them at some stages of our lives. Next time you find yourself in one, take a closer look at what's around you. You may be surprised at what you'll find.

The Chair
Genre: Horror

Agatha Burnell's favourite lumpy chair has been her saviour. But what secrets does it hold?

Royal Shopping
Genre: Comedy

A light-hearted look at what happens when the Queen goes shopping, finds a bargain, and doesn't seem to have the right change in her purse. Will anyone come to her aid?

Revenge
Genre: Comedy

There you are, not looking your best, and your ex-partner walks past with their new partner. How would you feel? Would you have revenge on your mind, or would you just laugh about it?

The Door
Genre: Paranormal

If somebody was calling for help from the other side of an old, scruffy looking door, would you go to their aid, or would you simply walk away?

The Wedding Bouquet
Genre: Drama

As a bride gets ready to throw her wedding bouquet to the eagerly waiting hands of her wedding guests, she asks the photographer to film the event. Will true love find the person who catches her wedding bouquet?

Fairies At The Bottom Of The Garden
Genre: Fantasy

Do fairies really exist? Roger Young, a cheating, lying, husband and father, is in for a colourful shock when he visits the greenhouse at the bottom of his garden.

Walking Into The Future
Genre: Drama

John Anderson has a dream of being able to walk into the future and finding out what awaits him. After completing the short journey, it's the journey back to his present that exposes a shocking truth.

Where To Now?
Genre: Science-Fiction

On the dying planet of Orion, the frightening events of what happened to all its inhabitants are revealed. Can what happened be stopped, before it spreads to other worlds?

The Whistle

~~~~~

When will it come? Every anticipated moment is like torture. Not even the silence that fills the dank air is comforting. I look to my left and see Jack, sat beside me. He looks as terrified as I do. I've known him for most of my life. We've grown up together and now, here we are, both terrified of what the future holds for us.

I want to cry, just like the dark sky above us. I look up and my eyes dart from left to right and then to the left again. Is this it? Is this really the reason why I've been born? Such a waste. I'm sure my mother didn't tell me anything about this. Why did she miss out this part of my life? I know that back at home she will be waiting patiently for any news of me. I feel so very sorry for her.

To my right, there's a slight movement. My body is frozen to the spot; all I can do is move my eyes in its direction. The face of a brown rat looks up at me. Twitching its nose, it's clearly wondering why I am here. Why we are all here. My eyes follow as it climbs across my legs before someone picks it up and throws it high behind me.

Nobody dares speak. It's like waiting for the end of the world. The whistle? When will it come?

I look down at my hands and remember the times my mother washed away the dirt under my fingernails. She would be so angry and want to wash them if she saw them now, but she would understand. I decide to move my left hand as pins and needles set in, only for it to be met by coldness as the numbness wears off.

My heart starts to beat faster when I feel something touch the little finger of my left hand. I dare not look down again for fear that the brown rat has returned. It may be as hungry as I am and want to gnaw away at my flesh. It wouldn't care that the fingernail of my little finger is dirty. Rats like dirt, don't they? Filthy creatures who desire nothing but darkness and fill us with fear.

As fast as the touch came, it disappears again. Should I look down to see if it's still there? What's the point? I ask myself. What's the point, because it won't be long before my life will end. I ask myself again, why did my mother never tell me anything about this part of my life?

The first drip of rain splatters on my face. Around me, I hear a few large drops finding their final resting places. It reminds me of the times that I loved to lie in bed listening to the sound of the rain on the roof. The rain was always my best friend. But, as quickly as those few large drops fall, they cease again and surrender to the stillness of the moment. The sky doesn't want to cry, not just yet. It, too, wants to hear the sound of the whistle. Yes, it can cry then, just like I will when the sound of the whistle comes.

The face of Justine appears right in front of me. She's beautiful. She's the prettiest girl around. Mother likes Justine and always compliments her on her choice of frocks and shoes. Laugh for me please, Justine. Laugh for me and take me away from here. I don't want to be here amongst the smell of rotting sandbags, stagnant mud, and the lingering odour of poison gas. I never wanted to come here. I want to hear your laughter and feel your soft kiss on my cheek. I want to smell the summer flowers and pick the fruits of autumn that are as sweet as you. I want to feed you blackberries and watch as you scrunch up your face because of their bitterness. Why did that always make me laugh? It was so cruel of me. I'm so very sorry.

I'd do anything to be able to tell you that I love you, Justine. Mother would be so pleased to know that. I can see my father now, shaking my hand and congratulating me on becoming a man, while my mother embraces you and welcomes you to the family. I wonder what our children would have been like? One girl and one boy, maybe? Now that can never be.

I have to let you go. It's not fair that you should wait for me. I'm never going to come back from here. I'm sorry to tell you that, but it's the truth. Fate has brought me here today. Fate always knew that I would end up here. The day I was born, Fate told Mother that I would be here, but Mother could never tell me. She would have cried had she told me. I don't like seeing Mother cry. Why was Fate so cruel to you, Justine? Why did it bring me into your life?

Was that the sound of the whistle? No. It can't be. It's still quiet and nothing moves. Is this the sound of Death I can hear? I wonder how Death will treat me as I walk up to it and look up and say who I am. Does Death know our names? I wonder how Death communicates with us? Does it have feelings like us? So many questions about Death which, no doubt, I will soon find the answers to. I hope Death treats me well. Please, Death, treat Justine, Mother, and Father kindly when they present themselves to you. Be kind to them. Don't make them suffer, as I am doing, now.

Something touches my little finger again and shatters the visions I have of Death. From inside, I start to scream. Was Death about to speak to me? Touch me? Was Death about to tell me its secret? No, please, Death, don't tell me your secret. If you tell me, then I know you will force me to tell you my secret. I can't ever tell you what it is. I can't even tell Mother or Father. Please, don't make me tell you. My secret has to be locked away and I must lose the key. I will hide it where nobody will ever look. Maybe I shouldn't worry about it. My secret can never get out of its prison for, if it did, then it would truly be the end of the world. But that would not matter to you, would it, Death? For you will always have a queue before you. You will always have people waiting to see you, wanting to be kind to you.

The taste of chocolate suddenly fills my mouth and I remember the chocolate bar in my pocket. Is there time to eat it before the sound of the whistle comes? I don't mind sharing it with you all. Like the loaf and five fishes, there will be plenty to go round. I promise you that we shall feast well before the whistle sounds. I remember how my eyes lit up when I saw that bar of chocolate for the first time. I'll save it for a special day, I told myself. Well, isn't today special? Isn't the day you are going to die special? No, maybe not. It's not as special as the day you are born or the day you first fall in love. Any day has to be more special than the day you die. Our Death day can never be special, but something tells me that today will be different.

The movement by my little finger comes again. I try and force myself not to cry as I realise that whatever touched my little finger never left. I have to look down this time. I have to stop asking myself all these questions and look down. Time is running out on us and I'll never forgive myself if I don't take a look.

I finally look down and see what it is that is touching me. Covered in dry mud, some of which is cracked and looks like the outlines of rivers on a map, I watch as the finger starts to move over my hand just like a caterpillar does when it explores. I'm mesmerised by it. It fascinates me and makes me so glad to still be alive. It stops short of the base of my little finger before moving around to its side. I watch as it raises itself up, as if it were a newly born creature that cannot open its eyes. I want it to wrap itself around me and I will it on to do so. Just as it starts to descend, the sound of the whistle stops it in its tracks.

Silence is shattered and all around me bodies start to move. I push myself up and await my turn. I turn to my left and, in front of me, Jack's hand finds its way towards me and squeezes my arm. I want to grab it and hold on tight, but it soon pulls away as somebody pushes Jack in a rush to climb up one of the ladders. Something heavy falls and knocks over the figures behind me, but I do not look as my eyes are transfixed on Jack climbing the ladder. The noise is now deafening, and fear has become king of the world around me. As I take my turn and climb the ladder, I wonder if Death awaits me on the other-side.

The sky finally begins to cry as I reach the top. Around me, plumes of smoke block out some of the bodies as they fall. I look for Jack and see him charging ahead through and over the barbed wire.

The thick mud makes it difficult for him to move fast as it sucks at his feet. I can't let him get away and I make my way towards him.

"Please, wait for me," I cry out, but he cannot hear me. My tears finally start to drain away from inside me. I don't want to lose him. Madness starts to descend, and I hear laughter all around me as I ask life not to be so cruel. If this is the day I am going to die, then let me do what I've so longed to do.

Beside me, somebody calls out, but the noise of the weapons drowns out their voice. I watch as a figure falls, his face hitting the soft mud and his eyes stare directly at me without ever moving again. Should I go to him and help? No, I remember what we were told. This is not a place for help. This is not a place for kindness. This is a place for survival, where one must only think of themselves.

I turn away from the man who stares at me and focus my eyes on Jack. I call out his name, but he carries on without me. Sadness engulfs me as I begin to think that he no longer cares for me. Many would say that what we have is a forbidden love, but we don't care about that. All we care about is being together. Trying to be alone together, without being discovered, is our biggest challenge. If we're ever caught, then society will disown us. They say that love conquers all, but I see no evidence of that here in the war-torn France of 1918. In fact, I see no evidence of it anywhere in England. Love may make the world go around but, sometimes, it does all it can to dislodge and destroy even the deepest parts of itself.

Just as the doubt of him ever loving me sets in, I watch as Jack falls towards the mud. Get up, I beg him. I stand there, not daring to move. Chaos may be all around me, but I cannot bring myself to move for fear of what I may find. I beg him to get up again, but still he refuses to move.

"BASTARD!" I shout, as I find all the strength in my body to take my legs towards him. "You bastard." My tears begin their conquest to match those of the sky. Sadness presents herself to me, but I refuse to look at her and let her win. Happiness is all we ever wanted. Where are you, happiness? It doesn't matter to us what others may think, for we always knew that we were born to be together. This is our love. This is pure love. And, do you know what pure love is? Pure love makes you feel like you are walking on the freshest of air. The type so pure that it has never been breathed in by another living soul. You can't leave me now, Jack. You are my life-raft. Without you, I will drown in the world that offers no hope of me ever finding love again.

I scream at the mud as it tries to suck me in and prevent me from reaching the man that I love. I won't let anything stop me from reaching him. He can't die alone, not without me. He can't die without anyone who loves him at his side. He doesn't deserve this. What did he do to deserve such a horrible life ending event as this? Is it my fault that his life is going to end like this? Was it my love that tricked him into taking this path? No, no, no! He deserves nothing but love as he leaves this world.

My body, now drained of energy, finally reaches him and I look down and watch the rain touch him. I don't want anyone or anything to touch my Jack. I fall to my knees and beg the world to stop so that time stands still and allows Jack to step back on. I want to say so much to this man who took my heart and who protected me from those that wanted nothing but to make my life a misery.

Was that a blink? Did he blink? I grab Jack's hand and tell him that I love him, but still he refuses to get up. He can't hear me. Of course, how can he hear what I am saying with all the noise? I lower my head and, as my lips touch his ear, I tell Jack that I love him and that I will never leave him. He gently squeezes my hand, and I know that he has not taken his love away from me.

The bullet enters my heart as I pull myself away from him. Jack closes his eyes as the upper half of my body falls towards the mud. My head falls next to his, and he takes one last look at me. I can feel him willing me to open my eyes, but it is too late. It doesn't matter to me that the bullet entered my heart because I know that Jack took it the moment before it entered. It's safe now.

The last thing I remember is that we are holding hands. It doesn't matter to either of us that anyone will see.

We both rise at the same time and look down at our bodies. Both at peace now, we begin a new journey together.

Upside-Down and Inside-Out

～～～～

According to Prudence Pebblebottom, there was no such thing as agoraphobia. How anybody could not force themselves over the threshold of their home to go on a date or to go shopping, she had no idea. Why the word 'agoraphobia' was in the Oxford English Dictionary, was beyond belief.

During a home visit when Prudence's mother, Beryl, was told by the doctor she was suffering from agoraphobia, Prudence was having none of it. The constant trying to force Beryl to go outside, while pushing her into the garden, was the cause of the heart attack that finally killed Beryl off. Of course, nobody knew what Prudence had done, but Prudence didn't care about that because she now owned the house as well as the £16, 262.82 in her mother's bank account.

Although the house was old, Beryl had kept it fairly neat and tidy. However, it still smelt of damp and mildew, but it was the constant dripping sound from a leaky toilet that finally persuaded Prudence that she needed to spend some of the money on home improvements. She could then sell up, downsize to a smaller home and, with the extra money, date younger men and spoil herself on shopping sprees and a world cruise.

A sudden noise from outside forced Prudence to go to the bedroom window. Looking down, Prudence was shocked to see the evil looking gargoyle, that had been attached to the top of the house, now on the ground, spewing out water, upwards, past the window like a fountain. But, like agoraphobia, it was not possible. There was only one thing for it: she'd have to go outside to try and make some sense of it.

On opening the backdoor, Prudence was shocked by what she saw. The sky seemed to be where the garden should be, and the garden was now above her, yet everything in the house was still the right way up. Trees and flowers hung upside down and a passing bird flew the wrong way up. A shower of raindrops went up instead of down and, upon putting her foot over the threshold of the door, there was nothing to support her.

Just like her mother had been, Prudence Pebblebottom was now a prisoner in her own home. Even though she didn't believe in agoraphobia, it had now not only turned her world upside-down but inside-out.

Baby Talk

~~~

We babies are smarter than you think. Sure, you won't remember when you were my age that you used to think and see the world like some of the adults, but that's because our memories are still under construction.

Anyway, on to the story I'm here to tell you.

There I was minding my own business, while out shopping with my mother, checking out the cool animals above me going round and round to the chime of 'rock-a-bye baby', when I overheard this conversation.

"Do you have anything for an itchy scalp?"

"Yes, madam, try this. It's made with coconut oil from the finest coconuts from the islands of The Bahamas. It will stop the itching."

"And what about something for helping me sleep?"

"Try this. It's made from our finest lavender oil. We grow the lavender ourselves at Kew Gardens. Add a few drops to your pillowslip before going to sleep, and you'll soon find yourself drifting off into a deep, relaxing sleep. It's guaranteed to help you get a good night's sleep, even during warm, humid nights and when having hot flushes."

"And what about something for my itchy legs?"

"Try this, madam."

"Oh, I like the bottle. It's cute. It's so soft to the touch. It feels like the skin on a newly born baby. What's inside?"

"Baby oil, madam."

"And what's it made from?"

~~

That was all this seven-month-old baby could take. I screamed the place down, and my mother ended up with just buying the coconut shampoo.

I hope we don't go back there again!

The Bag Lady

～～

"Is everything alright, Margaret?"

"Yes, I think so."

"Remember to keep the bag with you at all times."

"Yes, it's just that—"

"What?"

"Oh, I don't know. Don't take any notice of me. I'm just a bit overwhelmed, that's all. I really do feel as if I'm in London and it's 1975."

"That's because you are, and it is."

"But nobody can see me, can they?"

"No."

"Then why do I get the feeling that somebody is watching me?"

"Are they?"

"I don't know, I just get the feeling that somebody is."

"Well, look around you and see if anybody is taking a little bit too much of an interest in you. You're invisible, so they shouldn't be."

"Well, as long as you say so, Edith. Oh, there it goes again. The bag. It's vibrating. Does that mean I'm about to be transported home?"

"No. I want you to take one last trip for us, then you can come home."

"What? But why? I want to come back to 1961. Bert's tea needs cooking. I want to try out frying some sausages in my new Teflon-coated frying pan that he gave me for my birthday."

"It'll have to wait, Margaret. Take this one last trip for us, and we'll know then that everything is working."

"Well, if I must, but promise me you'll return me to four o'clock when I come back so that it gives me time to get Bert's tea on.

He wasn't very happy that I gave him cold meat and salad for his tea last night. He wouldn't let me watch Coronation Street. Where are you taking me this time?"

"To the year 1999. You'll be in London again, and you'll be looking for something called the Millennium Y2K bug."

"WHAT! Oh, you know I don't like insects and creepy-crawlies. Can't you send Gladys?"

"It's not an insect, Margaret. It's something to do with an invention known as computers and the internet—"

"Hairnet? What am I looking for a hairnet for? I've got lots of those at home."

"INTERNET! Oh, don't worry about it. Now listen to me. You should now be on your way to 1999. Hold on a moment, Gladys is trying to tell me something. You still have the bag with you, don't you, Margaret?"

"Yes, but something's not right, Edith."

"What do you mean?"

"Well, you know when you took me back to 1925?"

"Yes."

"Well, I knew then that I was invisible because nobody was looking at me. However, just now, in 1975, I had a feeling that somebody was watching me, and I could have sworn the same young man was watching me in 1947—"

"Are you sure? Why didn't you say so? We could have held you there a little longer before transporting you to 1999."

"Edith?"

"Yes."

"This time he most certainly is watching me. He can see me, and I'm sure he can hear every word I'm saying."

"What? Arc you sure?"

"Yes, I'm sure. It's the same young man who was watching me in 1975 and 1947. This time he seems to be dressed rather strangely."

"Walk away from him, Margaret, and see if he follows you."

"I can't."

"Why not?"

"Because I'm on the Tube."

"The Tube?"

"Yes. The London Underground. We're between stations. It's very busy and I can hardly move, but he's definitely watching me."

"You need to get off at the next stop and see if he follows you."

"Is that what you want me to do?"

"Yes, and, Margaret—"

"Yes."

"Keep the bag near you. Whoever he is, he may be after the bag."

"Why would he want the bag?"

"Why do you think he'd want the bag, Margaret? Haven't you just been time travelling?"

"Oh, yes. Well, I suppose if you put it like that, then yes, but why would he want the bag?"

"Stop asking silly questions. Do you want me to bring you back, so you can cook Bert's tea using that new Teflon-coated frying pan he gave you for your birthday?"

"Yes, but first I need to get it back off Gladys."

"Gladys? Why would our childhood friend and next-door neighbour have your frying pan?"

"Well— "

"STOP! Now listen, just do as I say. I don't know how that young man could ever think a seventy-one-year-old woman is a time traveller, but he must recognise the bag. Let's just say that you may not be the only time traveller. We never thought for a moment they would suspect a seventy-one-year-old woman, from the year 1961, as being a time traveller. It's probably what you're wearing that's attracted his attention, plus the bag, of course, because it has the built-in time travelling device. He'll want the bag, so he can sell it and make some cash. Mark my word, Margaret Jones, he wants the bag. Don't be surprised if he's been told to hunt down the Bag Lady."

"BAG LADY? That's not a very nice name to give your best friend, Edith Perkins. My Bert won't be happy with you when I tell him what you've just called me. You can forget about me giving you that recipe for Spotted Dick! Bag lady, indeed!"

"Shut up, Margaret! I'm not talking about you, I'm talking about the bag you're holding. It's called a Bag Lady. Gladys designed it in 1959 and it's one of only two in existence. Apart from the secret service for the over 60s, you and I are the only ones that know that Gladys was recruited specially to help hunt down people and viruses that may alter the timeline. On the day she was born, she was recruited by MI5 and—"

"You better not be having me on, Edith Perkins. My mother warned me about you. Be very careful, she told me, that one has trouble written all over her face."

"Is he still looking at you, Margaret?"

"Yes, but we're just pulling into a station. Hold on, while I try and make out which station it is. Umm…Kings Cross, we're about to stop at Kings Cross."

"Kings Cross? You're supposed to be going to Westminster. The crowds have gathered there to hear Big Ben chime in the year 2000. That's when the Millennium bug will strike."

"Then why didn't you transport me straight to 2000? I could then have told you if there are any hairnets."

"INTERNET, MARGARET, INTERNET! Don't you ever listen to what I say? Gladys is working on the problem. It seems the Bag Lady you have will only go as far as 1999. It must be faulty."

"How do you know that?"

"It's not important. What's important is that we get you to Westminster Station."

"I'm just getting off the train now. Doesn't look as if that young man is following me."

"Well, that's good news, but keep a lookout for him. According to Gladys, you've got several hours to go before Big Ben strikes midnight. I'm not sure why the device didn't take you all the way to just before midnight. I'll get Gladys to look into it."

"So, I need to get to Westminster?"

"Yes. Take the N20 or N5 bus to Trafalgar Square and you can walk from there. You'll have probably already noticed that London is a lot busier than it was in 1925, 1961, and 1975."

"I wouldn't want to still be living in London in 2000 and…err, what year did you say?"

"2000!"

"There are people everywhere. Oh, my goodness, I've just realised I don't have a ticket. How am I going to get past the ticket inspector?"

"He won't be able to see you, Margaret. Remember, you're invisible. Just walk straight past him. I've just remembered something Gladys told me. She said that ticket inspectors were replaced by automatic ticket barriers in the 1980s. You'll probably see them in the ticket hall as you exit the station."

"I'm going to board a bus, Edith. There are far too many people around for me to be walking all the way to Westminster, and the Underground is too busy. Besides, I'm hopeless with directions. I have to rely on Bert for getting us everywhere. My mother always said that navigation is a man's job. Don't ever try and tell a man he's going in the wrong direction, she told me. They may not want to stop and ask for directions, but he'll get you there eventually, and you'll gain some extra bingo nights by allowing him to think he's got you to where you're going all by himself—"

"Margaret!"

"Yes."

"Stop rambling on and listen to me! Gladys is going to try and fast forward you to 11:45. Where are you now?"

"Fast forward me? What do you mean? I've just reached the ticket hall. Shall I stop here?"

"No, you need to continue to get out of the station."

"But how am I to get through one of these strange barrier devices that allow people out of the station?"

"Hold on, I'll check with Gladys. Stay where you are. Remember, nobody can see you. Right, Gladys, how do we deal with this problem…Yes…ok…but are you sure it will work? Well…if you're absolutely sure, I'll inform her."

"Margaret?"

"Yes, Edith."

"There should be a large gate for prams and people with suitcases that you can go through. Just walk behind somebody going through that gate, and you can exit the station."

"Oh, my goodness! What the heck is happening? I don't like this, Edith. What are you doing to me?"

"Gladys is fast forwarding you to 11:45. Hold on, it won't take long."

"Arghhhhhhhhhhh! I don't like it. It's making me feel ill. Stop it now. Make it stop, Edith!"

"GLADYS! Turn it off…quickly. Margaret? Are you ok? Speak to me, please…Margaret?"

"Just a moment, Edith, my rain hood seems to have come loose."

"Where are you?"

"I seem to be sat on a bus."

"A bus?"

"Yes, a bus."

"Is it a bus numbered N20 or N5?"

"I don't know. How do I find out?"

"Look for clues. Are there any signs telling you what route the bus is taking?"

"I don't know. Everything is blurry. Let me put my specs on. Hold on…Arrgrrrrrrrrrr!"

"Margaret? Oh, my goodness, what's happened?"

"It's that young man. The one who can see me. The same one from 1947 and 1975. He's coming towards me."

"What? You have to run, Margaret. You need to get off the bus and get away from him. I'll try and get you back. GLADYS! Bring her back to 1961…Gladys? Where are you, Gladys?"

"Oh no, I've left the Bag Lady on the floor, Edith. Shall I go back for it?"

"WHAT?! Yes, go and get it. It's the only way we can get you back, Margaret!"

"Oh no! You're going to be so angry with me, Edith. The young man has picked the Bag Lady up and is coming straight towards me. Hold on, I'm going to tackle him."

"What? No!"

"Thank you, young man, but that's my Bag Lady. Now, kindly give it back to me or I shall have you taken to the school for naughty children, and you'll never eat ice-cream ever again!"

"Certainly, Mrs Jones, but you need to step off the bus with me… NOW!"

"I beg your pardon? Don't you speak to me like that, young man. You may be dressed strangely, but you're not too old to be put over my knee and…. hold on. How do you know my name? Get your hands off me…HELP! EDITH, HELP! Arrgrrrrrr!"

"Margaret! Are you all right? What was that sound?"

"I'm fine, Edith. It was Gladys hitting that young man over the head with my…just a minute. That better not be my brand-new Teflon-coated frying pan, Gladys Wilkinson!"

⁓

"Thank goodness Gladys got to you in time, Margaret. I don't think this time travelling malarkey is safe. Better go back to knitting and making jam. And, as for you, Gladys Wilkinson, no more Bag Ladies with built in time travelling devices! Now, who's for a nice cup of tea and a Custard Cream?"

The Tunnel

~⁓⁓~

It's been one of the most incredible journeys. Never did I believe that when we all went in, I'd be the only one to come out alive. There were lots of us when we went into the tunnel. None of us had any idea that not all of us would make it out again. I can see the light and hear muffled voices, so I think they're expecting me.

Getting ourselves ready to go in was full of excitement, because we all wanted the prize. I looked at the faces of all the other contestants, and they were as eager as I was. When the sign to begin the race came, we all went in as fast as we could. I'm not sure how many of us there were, but I'd heard rumours that in some of these races there were few competitors. I don't know if that's true, or if Simon was just trying to persuade me not to compete in this race so that he had a better chance of winning the prize. He may be my best mate, but he's also a bit of a slippery character.

Some of us had an advantage being at the front, but I found myself at the back of the pack. However, I went into that tunnel just as fast as the rest did. It got darker and darker the deeper we went in. I tried making my way to the front, but some were a lot stronger than I was. Still, I didn't give up.

At one point, Simon tried pushing me out of the way, but I was having none of it. I fought back and gradually made my way to the front. It was terrible when I saw the first casualties. I felt so sorry for them, especially Simon, but this was a race with a fantastic prize, and we had all been told that this journey was the survival of the fittest.

Despite the pitch darkness, those that were left knew the moment the prize was in sight. It was a strange object, something I'd not seen before, and it wasn't only me that dug deep for that extra bit of reserve energy I'd been saving. There was an almighty rush to get to it, not only because whoever touched the prize first got to keep it, but it would change their life forever. I don't know how I did it, but I pipped five others to the prize by a matter of milliseconds.

Now, just over nine months later, and with one last push, I'm about to escape this narrow tunnel and be born as a human.

Tiny People

～～

"Tell us exactly what you saw again, Mr Cumberland."

"But I've told you this story so many times. Doesn't anyone believe me?"

"It's not that we don't believe you; more that we find it hard to believe. You must know how important this discovery is…if it's true. Not only will it turn the whole industry on its head but the whole world."

Several more beads of sweat appeared on Max Cumberland's brow. Pulling down on his tie, he unfastened the top button of his sky-blue shirt while staring back at the middle one of the three interviewers sat in front of him.

"We've never been able to discover why the mobile phones started to smoulder before eventually catching fire. It has cost our organisation millions of pounds; as well as a huge downturn in sales. If what you are saying is true, then we would like to reward you. However, you have to be able to prove to us what you saw."

Max watched as the square headed man asking the questions pushed a mobile phone towards him. "It belongs to me. I haven't had any problems with it, apart from when my son sometimes plays with it, but perhaps you can check it and prove to us that what you discovered is true."

The square headed man smirked as he looked at both his colleagues sat either side of him. Max didn't like the way he smirked. It was the kind of smirk that said, 'you're an idiot'.

He knew all three would now study his every move.

"Take your time, Mr Cumberland, there's no rush," said the square headed man calmly, as he watched Max's shaking hand trying to remove the back of the phone.

With the help of a small tool Max had used to remove the cover from his own phone, a final click brought a huge sigh of relief. He smiled to himself before carefully removing the back of the square headed interviewer's phone, because he'd seen what he'd wanted to see on the screen of the phone. This was, at the time, the only model of phone that the game could be downloaded on.

The eyes of the three interviewers opened widely as events unfolded in front of them.

"Anything?" asked the square headed man.

Max carefully looked inside the mobile phone before removing its battery. Turning the phone in a clockwise direction, his eyes darted around looking for any signs of what he had discovered when he had opened the back of his own phone shortly after it had smouldered and caught fire.

Several minutes later, Max's heart pounded in his chest as he reinserted the battery before putting the phone down on the table. However, he kept the index finger of his right hand in contact with the edge of the phone before looking up towards the three interviewers.

"There were definitely tiny people inside my phone when I opened the back. It was 'them' that caused the phone to smoulder and catch fire."

The three interviewers laughed.

Unbeknown to everyone in the room, several tiny figures jumped from underneath the fingernail of Max's index finger and hid behind the battery.

"Put the cover back on the phone, Mr Cumberland. You've clearly wasted our time today. We'll contact you if we need you to come back," laughed the squared headed man.

∽

Later that day, at home, the square headed man sat down at the kitchen table. Having just taken a shower, he felt refreshed after such an appalling few weeks at work. His boss wanted answers as to why some of the mobile phones the company made were smouldering and he was giving the square headed man plenty of grief about it every day. Now it was his turn to work some of that grief off onto his wife and son. It wasn't right that they weren't feeling the distress he was getting.

Looking around the kitchen table, he noticed his phone was missing. He'd been certain he'd left it there when he had come in.

"Where's my phone?" he demanded of his wife, who was busy peeling potatoes at the kitchen sink.

"Billy has it. You said he could play that new game on it--"

"BILLY," screamed the square headed man, "BRING ME MY PHONE BACK, NOW!"

"You did say he could play with it—"

"I've told you before, don't speak to me unless I address you first. Do I make myself perfectly clear or do you need me to punish you again?"

For a moment, the potato peeling stopped, before it continued again, his wife too frightened to answer back.

"BILLY, I WON'T TELL YOU AGAIN, BRING ME MY PHONE, NOW!"

Apart from the scraping of potatoes, the house was silent, until the patter of feet could be heard coming towards the kitchen.

As soon as Billy entered the kitchen, the eyes of the square headed man dropped towards the phone in the child's hands.

"Who said you could remove the cover, boy?"

"Sorry, Daddy, it was the tiny people in the phone. They asked me to let them out. They said if I let them out, they'd help me."

"Tiny people? Help you?"

"The tiny people in the game. I asked them to help you, Daddy, so you wouldn't hit me or Mummy again."

For a moment, the square headed man could not believe what he was hearing.

"Are you having some kind of joke with me, boy? Tiny people? Who told you to say that?" he demanded, as he remembered the interview.

"They did, Daddy. The tiny people in the phone."

As rage built up inside him, the square head man bolted up from the table. The sudden movement was so strong that it caused the chair he'd been sitting on to smash against the kitchen wall, forcing one of the loose wooden legs to break and splinter. This, in turn, frightened Billy so much that he dropped the phone, breaking it into several pieces as it scatted across the black kitchen tiles.

"COME HERE, BOY," screamed the square head man, as he lurched forwards to grab the child. Billy, however, was already fleeing the kitchen in fear his father was going to hit him again.

As one of his bare feet made contact with some of the pieces of the phone and splinters on the floor, pain shot up the square headed man's left leg, forcing him to fall forwards towards the floor. His skull made a cracking sound as it hit the cold tiles.

Feeling slightly dazed, the kitchen seemed to spin around for a moment before his eyes saw the fluffy white slippers of his wife coming towards him. He'd never seen those slippers before. Where had she got the money to buy such expensive looking slippers?

The sudden noise of the potato peeler hitting the floor in front of his eyes not only stopped his line of thought, but shocked him, causing him to blink quickly. He tried moving his head but couldn't. He watched as his wife bent down to retrieve the potato peeler. Gripping the handle firmly, her hand froze for a moment.

Without warning, just before the potato peeler entered his right eye socket, he thought he saw several tiny figures. His ears picked up the faint words of '*do it*.'

⌇

Back in the lounge of the house, Billy carried on with downloading his favourite game, Tiny People, onto the phone his mother had secretly given him when he'd got home from school that same day. She'd been given the phone by somebody his mother referred to as 'Uncle Max'.

Billy had witnessed Uncle Max leaving the house quickly several times over many months but didn't want to tell anyone about it because it was 'their' secret, and the promise of a new mobile phone would not come true if he told anybody.

Not even the earth-shattering scream coming from the kitchen stopped Billy wanting to see the tiny people again.

Murder In Evershot

~~

John and I were with our dogs, Toby and Austin, in the little sleepy village of Evershot, in deepest Dorset, in the UK. We were there on a five-day break, but it could just as well have been St Mary Mead, home of Miss Marple, because that is what the place reminded me of.

I must admit that I've always been a big fan of Miss Marple. I've watched all the movies she's featured in, as well as all the TV shows. What I hadn't expected, though, was that I'd find myself involved in a murder mystery, the type of which only Miss Marple could have solved.

After dinner, on the first evening, as John and I were ambling past the vicarage on the way back to the inn where we were staying, walking Toby and Austin, I heard gunfire and somebody screaming. But maybe my mind was working overtime, or I'd had too much red wine with dinner.

During the night, I was woken by some noise coming from outside. Getting out of bed, and looking out of the window, I could have sworn I saw two, dark, shady figures carrying what looked like a rolled-up carpet. The light from the full moon helped me see them place it in the boot of a car that I hadn't since seen. Was this an unravelling mystery I'd stumbled upon?

The following morning, when we came down for breakfast, the heavy antique candlestick was missing from the dining room, and one of the cords, which had held a curtain back, was also missing, allowing the curtain to fall half way across the window.

One of the waitresses saw me looking at the curtain for far too long and informed me it was closed half way to block out the morning sun from some of the tables facing the window. It seemed like a simple enough explanation, but I still had my suspicions. As I walked past an open door leading to the kitchen, my stomach rumbled as the smell of fried bacon filled my nostrils. Taking a quick peek in, I was convinced I saw the chef holding what looked like lead-piping, but the thought of freshly baked Danish pastries from the self-service buffet stopped me from loitering for too long.

My goodness, this place really does feel like St Mary Mead, I thought, and I wanted to go and find which of the thatched roofed cottages Miss Marple lived in, so I could alert her to my suspicions. But, alas, I was informed by John that we had a full day booked out, so the visit to find Miss Marple would have to wait.

"You've an overactive imagination," he told me, as he tried refitting the loose name tag on Toby's collar.

When we got back from our day out, the events of the previous night and day were still heavy on my mind, and I was more determined than ever to find Miss Marple and tell her what I had witnessed.

As we took light refreshments in the bar at the inn, I asked the barman if he knew where Miss Marple lived. He looked at me in shock and shook his head quickly.

"I know of no such person living in the village," he cautioned. "Now, please excuse me as I need to replace the missing cord of the loose curtain in the dining room." He disappeared, leaving us alone in the bar, so we took our drinks to the beer garden.

When we finished our refreshments, John, Toby, and Austin all seemed tired and needed to rest. I took the opportunity to explore the village while they all took 'forty winks'.

Walking down the small high street, the late afternoon sun was still strong enough to make me feel hot and sweaty. A cool, fresh breeze forced me to turn right onto a small footpath that led to a few interesting looking buildings further down the path. I told myself that the thatched cottages towards the end of the path looked like the kind of place Miss Marple would live.

As I passed the first thatched cottage and glanced in the window, I was stopped in my tracks. On the windowsill was the very same antique candlestick, which had sat in the dining room of the inn the previous night. I'd admired it all evening, wondering how old it was and how much it was worth. Looking at it closely, I noticed how clean and shiny it was. Somebody had obviously taken a considerable amount of time cleaning it up, but they'd missed a small dark brownish spot at the base. Was it dried blood, or was it simply a blemish I was looking at? I took out my phone and took a photo of the candlestick. It could be used as evidence.

My attention was then drawn to the building opposite. It looked like a garage workshop from what I could see through a door, which was slightly ajar. I walked over and pushed the door open.

"Hello," I called out, but I was only met by silence.

Upon stepping into the workshop, I noticed an old motorbike, which lay disassembled across the floor. Lots of tools surrounded it. I walked over to it and immediately noticed some lead-piping propped up against the workbench. After taking a photo of the lead-piping, I took a handkerchief out of my pocket and picked it up, inspecting it closely. Could this have been the item used the night before on whoever it was rolled up in that piece of carpet? Then I noticed what looked like flakes of pastry stuck to one end of the piping. More evidence I could photograph. I was curious.

Placing the lead-piping back, I turned around. There was a loud bang and a scream, and my shirt suddenly felt wet.

I looked down. I'd been shot!

"Oh, Anthony! You are a naughty boy," shouted an old woman standing in front of me. "I'm so very sorry, Mr…"

"Roberts," I answered back, my eyes wide open by the shock of being shot.

"… Mr Roberts, you see, he thought you were a burglar. We were taken by surprise when we heard a noise coming from the workshop. I hope the water doesn't ruin your shirt. His father gave him the water pistol for his eleventh birthday, yesterday, and he's taken to firing water at everything. Can we help you? Perhaps you were looking for my nephew? Has he been repairing your car?"

"No, no, not at all," I said, "I was actually looking for Miss Marple. Do you know her? No, wait a minute, you're her, aren't…" I was interrupted by another loud bang and a scream, which seemed to come from the garden.

"Lucy! Will you be quiet! I've told you to stop popping those balloons," shouted the old woman.

Beside her, Anthony raised his water pistol and aimed it at me. I raised my arms in readiness for another blast of cold water.

"I'm sorry, dear, what did you say?" asked the old woman, as she faced me again.

"Miss Marple," I said, my arms still raised.

"No, dear, I'm not Miss Marple, I only wish I was."

"But you're dressed like her and look so much like her—"

"So many people get me mixed up with her," interrupted the old woman, who looked down her nose at me through a small pair of reading spectacles, and whose grey hair was tied into a small bun on the top of her head. "Why, if I'd had a pound for every time somebody asked me if I were Miss Marple, I'd be a very rich woman living near Harrods, by now. It's my favourite shop, you know…"

Clearly bored with hearing the old woman rambling on, Anthony made a quick exit and disappeared back into the garden.

"Now, how can I help you, dear, if it's not a car or anything else my nephew has repaired for you? Would you perhaps like a cup of tea or a glass of lemonade to get over the shock of Anthony shooting you?" She paused, looked at me and, before I knew it, she was escorting me into the large garden, where we sat around a big metal garden table that had a tall, bright yellow sun umbrella protecting us from the hot, late afternoon sun. Though it was only partly covering me; the old woman had taken the sole chair in full shade.

While Anthony and Lucy chased each other around the garden, popping balloons and occasionally getting wet from the water pistols they both had, I told my story of the events of the night before while the old woman listened intensely, drank tea, and ate cucumber sandwiches. She seemed somewhat interested in my mobile phone, so I decided to show her the photos I'd just taken of the candlestick and lead-piping.

"Why do you have so many photos on your phone, especially of doors? Do you really find doors interesting?" she enquired, as I revealed my photo gallery on my phone.

"Those are for a photography challenge I sometime participate in on my blog," I replied.

"You have a blog? Oh, please show me."

For the next twenty minutes, I showed her some of my blog posts, photos of Toby and Austin, as well as a photo I'd taken of the front door to our house. She seemed very interested in everything, but especially the photo of our front door.

'Is that Welsh slate your house number is on next to the door? I so love Welsh slate. Are you on Facebook too? I'd love to see more photos of where you live. Swansea sounds a lovely place to visit."

She seemed to be taking a mental note of everything I was showing her and everything I was saying, but it didn't bother me. She was, after all, going to solve the mystery I'd been telling her about.

"Now, about the incidents I've witness…" I announced, as she cut into a homemade Victoria Sandwich cake with a rather frightening, vintage bone handled knife. I watched as the jam and butter icing oozed out of the sides and, by the time I'd finished my sentence, she'd shoved a huge piece towards me. I felt it rude not to try some.

"Oh, my dear, your story all sounds very tragic and nothing like what goes on here in the village," she announced, while still holding the knife in her hand. She then seemed to go into deep thought.

Suddenly, I started to feel ill and my vision became slightly blurred. I rubbed my eyes and closed them tightly before opening and closing them several times hoping the blurriness would correct itself. I then began to wonder why the old woman had not offered any of the cake to Anthony or Lucy or eaten any herself. A sudden horrible thought came into my mind. Had she poisoned me?

The last thing I remembered before passing out was seeing the old woman coming towards me, the knife still firmly in her hand.

~~

The first thing I saw, when I opened my eyes again, was John looking down at me. Toby then popped his head up by the side of me and licked my face. I noticed that his name tag was missing off his collar again, while Austin gave me an encouraging 'bark'.

"Where am I?"

"Back at the inn," replied John. "Are you feeling better? You gave us all a scare."

"Oh no, where's that old woman I was talking with? I'm sure she poisoned me."

"Oh, don't be silly," replied John, "we have a date with her and the rest of the village in the downstairs bar in half an hour. She has some important news for you. Are you feeling well enough to come down for some dinner and to meet everyone?"

After taking a shower, I was feeling much better and hadn't realised that I'd passed out for about two hours. John informed me that he had been out looking for me while walking Toby and Austin, when they had heard a call for help from the garden where I had passed out. They'd managed to get me back to the inn, although I could not recall any of it. The local doctor had paid me a visit and declared that I had a slight case of sun-stroke.

I was quite nervous walking downstairs to the bar; I almost felt embarrassed by what had happened, but John told me that the mystery of the 'Murder in Evershot' was about to be solved.

Everybody in the bar seemed to know that I had passed out; they were all very concerned. I managed to eat something and was told to drink plenty of fluids while the other residents of the village gathered in the bar. Twenty minutes later, everyone, apart from the old woman, was present.

"She's not going to arrive, is she?" I asked.

"She'll be here. I promise," replied John. "Besides, she's the one with all the answers."

As if by magic, the old woman suddenly appeared in the doorway of the bar. The hairs on my arms stood up in fear, and I suddenly felt cold and shivered. She looked at everybody around the room, glancing last at me. A smile appeared across her face.

"I'm so glad you are feeling better, Mr Roberts. Let me solve this mystery for you and put your mind at rest once and for all. I've spoken with the staff here at the inn, and various residents of the village, and what I am about to tell you and everyone else here this evening will all make perfect sense."

She walked towards me in complete silence. Even the sound of the birds singing their evening chorus outside seemed to stop.

"I'll be very frank with you and everyone else here, Mr Roberts. You see, it's all very simple, so let me begin."

She picked up a fresh glass of water from a table, took a few sips, and coughed to clear her throat.

"The dark, shady figures you saw carrying the rolled-up carpet to the car. It's very simple, my dear. As you know, this inn is dog friendly. After all, it's the only reason you and John booked to stay here, so you could bring Toby and Austin. Accidents happen and, unfortunately, one of the other resident's dogs had made rather a nasty mess on some carpet in the lounge after you'd gone to bed, so the carpet had to be taken away. The lounge was closed while some of the staff moved furniture around, so the carpet could be lifted. It was a long job and they did not want to disturb any of the residents, so the carpet was removed just after midnight. All you saw, that night, Mr Roberts, was a member of staff putting a rather soiled piece of carpet in the back of a car."

"But I haven't seen the car since last night," I pointed out.

"That's because the car belongs to a member of staff who has been off-duty today. Please, don't interrupt, Mr Roberts, there will be plenty of time for questions once I finish."

She took another sip of water.

"As for the antique candlestick, it was on loan to the inn for a wedding held here a few days ago. It belonged to Mrs Peacock, who cleaned it up when she got it back. The dark spot you saw when looking at it through her window was simply a food blemish. Her eye sight is poor, and she'd not worn her spectacles when cleaning it, so she had not spotted the blemish."

The room remained silent. Nobody took their eyes off the old woman.

"The missing curtain cord was another dog related mystery. It was found in the bed belonging to the very same dog who had soiled the carpet in the lounge. It seems Rosie has a liking for ropes and cords as she loves to play 'tug-of-war' with her owner."

There was some laughter in the room before she continued.

"Now, on to the lead-piping you discovered in my nephew's workshop. He's a part-time chef here at the inn. In fact, he makes the Danish pastries along with Mrs White, the Head Cook. He brings home any leftovers. They are delicious, and he often eats them when working on repairing cars and motorcycles. However, what you saw him with that morning when you walked past the kitchen was a black pudding. After all, you do enjoy the full English breakfast here at the inn, don't you, so what would a full English breakfast be without black pudding?"

She smiled at me and continued.

"Murder at the vicarage…the gun shot and the scream you heard as you walked past last night? Quite simply the Reverend Green, his granddaughter, Miss Scarlet, and his neighbour, Professor Plum, all watching a murder-mystery on the fifty-inch television screen with sound boom-bar left to the vicarage by Colonel Mustard, on his sudden departure to go and live in Canada. So, there you have it, Mr Roberts, mystery solved."

There was a large round of applause, and the room became alive again. Even the evening chorus, outside, resumed.

"Now I must leave and be on my way," announced the old woman. "I've had a call from my sister in St Margaret Mead, informing me of a strange mystery that has something to do with a strange subject that goes by the name of 'writer's block'. I've never heard of it before, but I do enjoy solving a mystery."

"But before you go, I must thank you for solving this mystery for me," I announced.

The old woman turned around and gave me a smile I knew I'd never forget.

⌇

You won't be thanking me for long, thought the old woman, as she turned around and faced Hugh. You tourists are so foolish. You all come here thinking this place is something to do with Miss Marple, because of the way it looks, and the way I dress, and you become putty in our hands.

Walking out of the bar, the old woman fumbled around inside her expensive handbag for the car keys to her Porsche. The residents of the village had once again done a splendid job of staging a murder mystery and would all be well rewarded. Once inside her car, she opened up the compartment inside the centre armrest and removed the tag she'd taken from the collar of one of the dogs when John had come into the garden. He hadn't noticed her removing the loose tag, while attending to Hugh. It was the final piece to the jigsaw she needed for her next job.

"My name is Toby. I'm microchipped," she read out, as she held the tag up and looked at it.

"Yes, and your missing tag also gives me the postal code of the home you and your owners live in," she muttered, as she punched the postal code into the car's satellite navigation system. "And as one of your owners also revealed to me where you live and showed me the photo of the front door with the lovely numbered Welsh slate, I now know exactly which house I can break into and rob tonight. You tourists never learn, do you?" she laughed.

Floral Hall

~~~

"Are you OK, Mum?"

"Yes, I'm fine, Hilary. I'll just sit down here for a while and rest my eyes while you go and catch up with Tim and Barney."

"OK, I won't be long," replied Hilary, as she walked off, calling out for her young son.

Margaret closed her eyes, and it was not long before the presence of somebody else sitting down beside her on the bench disturbed her.

"Shall we dance?" came the words. She opened her eyes and smiled. It was about time he asked her to dance after all these weeks. She held out her hand to him, and they both stood up and walked towards Floral Hall.

~~~

"Barney," called out Hilary. Tim held his mother's hand as a black Labrador dog came bounding towards them. "Here, boy, there's a treat for you." Tim let go of his mother's hand and walked towards the building just to their right, while his mother attempted to get Barney on his lead. However, the dog was having none of it and thought it a game.

"Come away from there, it's not safe."

"Mummy, I can hear music coming from inside," shouted Tim.

"Don't be silly, darling, that building was closed down and boarded up years ago. It's where your grandmother and grandfather first met. They used to go dancing there every Saturday night."

Tim pushed his ear up to a piece of board. He was sure he could not only hear music but the sound of people laughing and talking as well. A cold, wet nose on his leg disturbed the moment, and he saw Barney looking up at him, wagging his tail.

"Come on, we have to get back to your grandmother. It would have been Grandad's eightieth birthday today, and we have to visit his grave."

With the sound of music and laughter now having disappeared, Tim made his way back to his mother. Barney was a few steps behind him.

"There was music coming from inside the building," said Tim.

"Don't be silly, darling. Come on, let's get back to your grandmother."

They walked towards Margaret who still had her eyes closed.

"Are you OK, Mum?" called out Hilary.

~~

Margret kept her eyes closed, for she was no longer sat on the park bench. Instead, the sound of music filled her ears, and the scent of her husband's aftershave filled her nostrils, as they both danced around Floral Hall.

"Happy eightieth birthday," were Margaret's final words.

The Right Choice

～ ⌣ ～

Stacey and Carl entered the old ruins – and were never seen again...

～

Twenty-four hours earlier.

"Stacey and Carl, is it to be the killer bees or the old ruins? The choice is yours, but you only have twenty seconds to make up your mind as to which one you will face. For one million pounds, you need to make the right choice. Come on, ladies and gentlemen," said the gameshow presenter, "let's give them some encouragement while the clock counts down. Are we ready? Start the clock!"

While the audience cheered, the clock counted down, and the TV cameras focused on Stacey and Carl who were outside on location. Behind them, some old ruins stood at the top of a steep grassy hill.

Nineteen seconds - Stacey looked at Carl.

Eighteen - "What should we do?" she asked.

Seventeen - The sweat on Carl's forehead started to sting his eyes.

Sixteen - "CARL! WHAT DO WE DO?"

Fifteen - Carl found himself frozen to the spot.

Fourteen - "I can't face bees, Carl. They terrify me."

Thirteen - Carl started to feel sick.

Twelve - "The bees or the old ruins?" asked Stacey.

Eleven - "Which one should we choose, Carl?"

Ten - Carl looked at Stacey but couldn't open his mouth.

Nine - "SAY SOMETHING, CARL!"

Eight - Carl looked up at the old ruins.

Seven - "The old ruins?" asked a terrified Stacey.

Six - Carl nodded his head.

Five - "Are you sure?"

Four - Carl thought he could hear the first sound of the killer bees approaching.

Three - Carl grabbed Stacey's hand.

Two - "Now!" He pulled Stacey with him.

One - They started the climb towards the old ruins.

Zero - The sound of a gong. The audience cheered.

"Ladies and gentlemen, our contestants have made their choice, but is it the right choice? Will they find the million pounds prize inside those old ruins? We're about to find out."

A few moments later
as Stacey and Carl reached the old ruins.

"I think we made the right choice, Carl. Look, it seems safe in here and there's no sign of the bees. Look for the money. They said it would be in a brown leather case."

They started searching the old ruins, and Carl soon spotted a brown leather case. He pointed it out to Stacey. The audience went silent.

"WE'VE DONE IT!" screamed Stacey, as she ran towards the case and lifted it up. Triggering a trap, the floor of the old ruins opened up and both plunged to their deaths. The audience gasped and were shocked…but not for long.

"Ladies and gentlemen, that means next week's prize money rolls over to…two million pounds," jeered the gameshow host.

The audience cheered.

"Now, without further ado, let's welcome today's special guests… The Killer Bees, who are here to sing their new single which is being released tomorrow."

The audience whooped as the band came out on stage, holding a brown leather case, and began singing their new song, 'The Right Choice'.

Knock, Knock

❧

"**K**nock, knock."
    "Who's there?"
    "Let me in, or you're dead."
"What?"
"Knock, knock."
"Who's there?"
"Let me in, or you're dead."

"Look, I'm not playing this game. You're scaring me and my little sister. My parents will be home soon, so you better go, otherwise Papa will punch you on the nose."

"Knock, knock."

"I told you, you're scaring me. I'm not playing this game anymore."

"Let me in, or you're dead."

"No! I'm not letting you in. Go away…PLEASE!"

For the next sixty-six seconds, there was nothing but total silence until, out of curiosity and as the clock struck six, Angela opened the door and peered out into the garden. Whoever it had been was gone and all seemed normal. That was until Angela turned to close the door. Where had the door knocker gone? Surely whoever had been using it to knock on the door hadn't stolen it? Then again, she'd always hated the knocker. Shaped as the head of a horned devil, it had always frightened her. They were welcome to it.

Taking a few quick steps backwards into the house, Angela felt safe again.

"Knock, knock," came a voice from the right of Angela.

Unable to move, she watched as a hand of evil slammed the door shut, and her little sister screamed.

Fast Forward

⌒⌒⌒⌒

I certainly hadn't noticed the new feature when I purchased the smart watch. Not even the sales assistant had mentioned it to me. Now, here I was, very excited by the prospect of what it might do. Of course, it probably wouldn't do much and was a cheap gimmick and, like most other people, I hadn't bothered reading the instruction booklet.

The new watch vibrated whenever a new email arrived or somebody, somewhere, on social media had mentioned me by name. I loved both the look of the watch and the colour of the strap I had chosen. Sky blue was my colour because it matched the colour of my eyes. Being a red-head, I had to be so careful with my choice of colours. The red strap would never have suited me.

I needed a cup of tea and, while waiting for the kettle to boil, I decided to go back and sit at my desk. I hadn't taken much notice of the dial on the side of the watch. After all, it was kind of old-fashioned, and I had only turned it because the time was incorrect. The eleven o'clock news had just started on the radio, yet my watch showed a time of 10:37.

Turning the dial forward, I watched as the time changed but, to my amazement, as I looked up, the trees outside my study window blew as if they were on fast forward. I stopped turning the dial and looked down at the time on the watch, which now showed 11:29. That was when I remembered that I'd put the kettle on to boil, so I made my way back to the kitchen to make the cup of tea I had promised myself without correcting the time to 11:00.

But not only was the water in the kettle only lukewarm, the DJ on the radio announced that the time was 11:30 shortly after

I entered the kitchen. What? How could that be? It didn't make sense. I looked at the watch and, sure enough, it showed the time as being 11:30. I immediately had the urge to turn the dial again. This time, however, and to ensure I wasn't dreaming, I moved it fast forward several times so that I could find out if I would end up in tomorrow.

"I'll be late home this evening," were the first words I heard when I stopped moving the dial forward. It almost made me jump out of my skin. There, sat at the kitchen table and eating breakfast, was my girlfriend, Annabelle.

"Did you hear what I just said, Brad? You're taking a little bit too much interest in that new smartwatch."

Dumbfounded, I didn't know what to say. Was Annabelle a figure of my imagination? Was she really sat in our kitchen eating breakfast? I walked towards her and pinched her on the arm.

"Ouch! Why did you do that?"

"What's the date?" I laughed, "is it April Fool's day?"

"The date? April Fool's? Why are you asking those silly questions? Doesn't that new watch tell you what the date is? If it's faulty then I'd take it back to the store. Why did you just pinch me?"

"Was I wearing these clothes yesterday?" I asked.

"What? What's got into you, Bradley? I think you need to get out a bit more. Sitting in front of the computer, writing all day, is obviously having a serious effect on your health. What on earth is wrong will you?"

This time I was unable to answer Annabelle's questions, because I didn't have the answers. I just looked at her as if I didn't have a clue what she was saying. No wonder she got fed up and went to work without finishing her breakfast. She didn't even kiss me or say goodbye.

As usual, I cleared away the breakfast dishes and noticed there were two mugs, two bowls, two plates, and two spoons and knives. I'd obviously been eating breakfast with her, but my mind was now working overtime as to what on earth had just happened. It was only when one of my favourite songs started playing on the radio that my mind was taken off things for a while. In fact, all memories of what had just happened seemed to fade fast and it wasn't until the watch on my wrist vibrated that I remembered something about turning the dial and how it had somehow made me jump a day.

"What a cool plot for a new short story," I said out loud. I quickly made my way to my study and turned on the computer. The watched vibrated again and displayed a message that somebody had just left a comment on one of my blog posts. I always dealt with emails first before responding to comments left on the blog and, for the next hour, I dealt with both before finally opening a new document to start writing the story.

Tea first, I told myself after writing the opening line, then I'd get on with writing. This time, I stood next to the kettle while I waited for it to come to the boil. I looked at my watch and saw that it was 09:56. I pushed the dial forward slowly so that the time moved to 09:59 and took my hand away. Shocked, I watched as the kettle suddenly switched itself off. I touched the side of the kettle and immediately pulled my hand away. The water had boiled, but I was now more concerned and excited that I seemed to have been able to move myself forward in time again.

I looked around the kitchen and, other than the clock on the far wall displaying that it was ten o'clock, everything else was the same. I smiled to myself and started moving the dial on the watch forward again. I watched, gobsmacked, as I saw myself come in and out of the kitchen as if I was on fast forward. It only stopped when I had to move my finger and thumb back to move the dial forward again. I kept moving the dial and watched as Annabelle came home. She kissed the new me that had appeared, and I watched as we made supper together and ate the meal quickly. Everything seemed to be on fast forward.

I turned my head towards the window and watched as the light faded and nightfall came. The lights in the kitchen came on and then went off again. I kept turning the dial and watched as the time on the kitchen clock moved forward. Daylight finally broke again, and I decided to move the dial even faster.

It was like being on the dance floor of a nightclub as the strobe lighting of days and nights flashed by quickly. Everything was now moving so fast that I began to feel dizzy. That's when I stopped turning the dial and almost fell over.

"Come on, mate, where's the pizza?" called out a voice. There was only me in the kitchen, but the sound of a football game on the TV was coming from the lounge.

"Hurry up! What does a guy have to do to get a beer around here?" came a voice that I recognised.

"Adrian?" I called out.

"Yeah?" came back the reply.

I looked at the time on the kitchen clock. 15:07. My watch showed the same time. I then looked at the date just to the left of the time. *Sat 29 Oct*. What? That was over a month away. Why was my watch showing a date over thirty days away?

"What the heck are you doing, mate?" asked Adrian, as he walked into the kitchen, dressed in his Cardiff City football shirt and a matching pair of jeans. "We're missing the match. Where's the pizza? Did you get any more beers in?" I just stood there, not able to say anything. "Are you okay, mate? You look like you've seen a ghost."

"You can see me?" I asked. Adrian looked at me weirdly.

"I think you've had one too many beers, mate. Where are they? In the fridge?" he asked, as he walked towards the fridge, while I stood there not able to move.

"Jeez, mate, you've not even put the pizzas in the oven yet, they're still in here. What have you been doing out here?"

Adrian looked at me, waiting for a reply, but I couldn't do anything other than try and figure out if what was happening to me was real. I then looked down at the watch and decided to push the dial forward a little so that the time displayed 15:31. When I looked up, Adrian was gone, but I could hear him cheering from the lounge.

It was at this point that I started to become a little concerned. What the heck was going on? My finger and thumb reached for the dial to get me out of the situation as quickly as possible.

Closing my eyes, I moved the dial forward. I was slowly becoming terrified at what was happening to me and just wanted to get back to the moment before I had first turned the dial. You should be moving the dial back, said a voice in my head, yet the thought of what lay ahead further into my future had me both overcurious and thrilled at what was to come. All the questions I'd started asking myself when I'd heard Adrian cheering from the lounge disappeared. Instead, I remembered how as a child, I'd always wanted to time travel into the future after watching the time traveller in H.G. Wells' movie, 'The Time Machine'.

As I kept moving the dial forward, I told myself a few more trips into the future wouldn't hurt. If I became terrified again, then I would simply turn the dial backwards and take the watch back to the shop and get a refund. If they wouldn't refund me my money, then they could jolly well tell me what the heck was going on with this time travel function and why nobody had mentioned anything about it. I felt like crying but kept telling myself that this was probably a silly nightmare, and that Annabelle would wake me up any moment to tell me I was having a bad dream.

I don't know what it was that made me stop moving the dial and open my eyes quickly but, when I did, I was startled. At least eight pairs of eyes stared back at me. The faces were old, well-aged, and mostly covered in wrinkles. They did nothing but stare at me. Then I realised that all my surroundings had changed. I wasn't at home anymore but in a large lounge I didn't recognise. My eyes started to scan the room quickly. There were quite a few people, mostly old women, sat in the room. I could see an old man asleep in a chair. He drooled, as I watched a younger woman, dressed in a light blue overall and an old-fashioned nurse's hat, come into the room, wipe the drool from his mouth, and place a blanket over his legs.

On a wall, to my left, was a strange looking screen that seemed to be broadcasting a wedding. I couldn't hear the sound, but subtitles were flashing across the bottom of the screen. The titles said it was the Royal Wedding of the grandson of King William and Queen

Katherine. It looked like a news broadcast, but I decided that it must be a movie. William and Kate were far too young to have a grandson.

"Hello, Bradley dear. How are we today?" asked a voice I seemed to recognise. "I see you still have the watch on. How old is it now?"

I looked down at my wrist first before looking up at the aged figure of Annabelle, stood in front of me. I was shocked by what age had done to her. I could make out crow's feet at the side of her eyes, while her hair was as grey as most of the old women sat in the room. Although her fashion sense had not changed; I knew immediately that many people would probably think she was mutton dressed up as lamb.

"Would you like some tea? You need to keep your fluids up. You know what the doctor said. I'll get you a cup, shall I? Would you like a biscuit as well? I'm sure I saw some of those chocolate bourbons we used to like."

I watched as the figure turned and walked towards a large table containing lots of cups and saucers, a large teapot, and a small stack of plates. She poured milk from a dainty jug covered in red and gold flowers before lifting a matching teapot and pouring tea into two cups.

"Would you like a cup, Barbara?" she asked.

"No, thank you. I've just had my break," replied the woman who had just wiped the face of the old man asleep in the chair.

"Not a bad day, is it? They say the good weather is set to last all week. I hope it does, so we can celebrate my Bradley's 80th birthday in the home's garden."

"I hope so, Annabelle, but you can never trust the British weather, can you?" laughed Barbara.

"How's he been?" Did he get a good night's sleep?"

"I think so. Julia, who was on night duty last night, didn't say anything before she went off shift this morning, so he must have slept well."

"Oh, that's good. The doctor did say that some patients with dementia sleep well. I think Bradley is one of those. He was never a good sleeper. I put it down to all the writing he did. Did I tell you that he's had over twenty books published?"

'Yes, I think you did mention it."

That was all the conversation I could bear to hear before I closed my eyes and pushed the dial of the watch forward again. However, this time, pushing the dial seemed to be more difficult for me. It was hard work, and it wasn't long before I gave up.

When I opened my eyes again, I was in complete darkness. Was I dead? It was the first thought I had, yet I was sure I could hear the muffled sound of singing. Although I felt very weak, I tried moving my arms. I managed to move them to the side a little but no further. Then I remembered the watch and hoped it was still on my wrist. I didn't like this place at all and wanted to get back to the kitchen. It was time to turn the dial in the other direction and go back.

I don't know why, but as soon the singing stopped and I heard the muffled voice of a man, I thought back again to the time traveller in the movie. Like him, all I'd wanted to do was travel into the future, but it was now time for me to travel back to the kitchen, where I'd started. As I tried moving my left hand over to my right wrist, so I could turn the dial backwards, everything around me started to shift.

I began to panic as I tried desperately to move my left hand to the watch, but I was too weak. Before I knew it, I was moving headfirst at a slow pace. I could hear some music, and as I tried to scream out, my voice refused to work.

It was still pitch black, and I felt as if I were in an elevator, only in a horizontal position rather than a vertical one.

My voice still refused to work as the flames engulfed me and my coffin.

The Jump

Jane Collins' worst fear was to be buried alive. It was one of two things that woke her up during the night. The nightmare was so vivid: she would wake up in complete darkness, not able to move, struggling to breathe. Her skin felt clammy but, worse still, her armpits were stuck together like glue.

If it wasn't the nightmare of being buried alive, then it was Roland's snoring that woke her. How could she have fallen in love with him and accepted his proposal of marriage so quickly? The very thought of his hot, clammy, sticky body on top of hers as he tried to make love to her, made her feel sick to the stomach. But although Roland was almost twice her age, he was a rich man, and although she denied it, it was the money that was the attraction.

The knowledge that Roland worshipped her kept Jane safe. He hadn't even said anything to her when she'd spotted him looking through the restaurant window one evening while she was having dinner with Steve, her lover of the past four years. Steve was only ten years older than her and kept himself fit by working out at the gym every day. His blue eyes, blond hair, pert bottom, and die-for smile made every woman want him and every man want to be him.

She had told Roland that she was away on business, yet all she was doing was spending another passionate night with Steve in the Carlton Hotel on the other side of the island. She was tempted to ask him about it when she returned home the next day. However, Jane decided that the money was too important.

Knowing Roland's only fear was that of heights, Jane had decided she would give him a parachute jump for his 50th birthday. She wanted to see just how far she could push him, and how far he would go to please her.

"I'll only jump if you jump with me," Roland said to her after he opened the gift. It was no problem for Jane, because heights didn't scare her and there was no chance of being buried alive while falling from the sky.

On the day of the jump, Jane had it all planned out. She'd persuaded Steve, and Roland himself, that the latter didn't need an instructor strapped to him even though it was his first jump. She promised Steve that she would bail out his unsuccessful extreme sports business if he also saw to it that Roland's parachute didn't open. And the final clincher – she would marry Steve and they could enjoy Jane's entitlement from Roland's estate. She'd made sure the will hadn't been changed and that everything would still go to her. She and Steve could then live happily ever after on their island paradise.

Jane watched as the beads of sweat rolled down Roland's face. They were nearing the point where they were going to jump out of the plane. Making a 'thumbs-up' sign to Roland, the instructor, who had been bribed with some of Roland's money, spoke to them though their headsets.

"Ready?" he asked.

Jane nodded, while Roland looked terrified.

"We're ready," called out the instructor to the pilot, who had also been easily taken in with a bribe.

"You'll be fine, darling, I promise you," Jane assured Roland. "Do it for me. You know how much I love you. Just look at the beautiful view out there. The Island looks like paradise, doesn't it?"

Roland nodded, but couldn't bring himself to speak or look out of the window.

"Are you ready, Roland?" asked the instructor. "You're going to have a great time."

'Come on, darling," beckoned Jane, "watch me jump, and you follow, ok?"

As Jane dangled her feet out of the plane's hatch, she looked down. Soon, the beautiful island below would contain her and Steve as a married couple. Her paradise would be complete. Then, for no reason, the thought of being buried alive crossed her mind. She shuddered and shuddered again when she turned her head towards Roland, watching as he wobbled his way forward to the hatch. He was actually going to do it. At last, it was going to happen, and she would soon be rid of him.

She hesitated before jumping as the shape of the island below her seemed to change slightly. Not only that, but the whole texture of the island looked a little different. As Roland sat behind her, she turned her attention away from the island and towards him again. He was really going to do it. He was going to do it for her and give her the life she so wanted with Steve. As the instructor counted down from five to one, she gave Roland the 'thumbs-up' before jumping out of the plane.

She was free at last. Free from the plane, free from her current life, and free from Roland. Down below her, a new life with Steve awaited. As she took in the views of the island and the clear waters that surrounded it, Jane's heartbeat accelerated. She felt as if a whole weight was being lifted off her shoulders as she fell through the air.

With her eyes fixed on the island, Jane's mind started to go into overdrive as she tried to work out why the island didn't look the same as it had done when she had first looked out the plane's window. She'd flown over the island many times before, its shape and texture from the sky etched onto her mind, yet here it was now looking somehow different. As she descended to the point at which she needed to deploy her parachute, she wondered how far Roland was behind her.

Pulling the handle, Jane's mind focused on the job at hand, and her body went into a vertical position as the opened parachute pulled her up into the sky. She immediately started to look around her for any signs of Roland but couldn't see him anywhere. He can't have made the jump, she thought. The bastard hasn't made the jump!

Damn him, her plan had failed. As a huge feeling of disappointment took over her body, Jane looked around for the plane, but it was nowhere in sight.

Trying to make sense of where the plane and Roland were, Jane continued to float towards the island. They'd been told which part of the Island to land on yet, as the landing site came into view, it didn't look the same. Instead of a huge open area of grassland, there was now something dark and uninviting. Where on earth was she? Had she jumped out of the plane at the wrong time? Was this one of the uninhabited neighbouring islands?

Just before landing, Jane realised that she'd also seen no evidence of any boats or ships in the sea. As she neared the ground, she could see she was about to land in a boggy area. Doing all she could do to get away from it, she manged to land right on its edge. However, the quicksand soon took its hold of the lower part of her body.

As the quicksand tried to suck her in, Jane's nightmare of being buried alive quickly came back to her.

"HELP!" she called out. "STEVE, HELP ME!"

Steve was supposed to be here, the area where he'd told her to land. "STEVE!"

A sudden movement behind some thick vegetation stopped Jane's struggle.

"Is that you, Steve? Help me, please. I'm being sucked in."

Jane's eyes widened as a number of figures holding spears and shields stepped out from behind the vegetation. Dressed only in reeds that hung down from their waists, the figures made their way towards her. Pale skinned and each wearing matching necklaces that looked like pieces of teeth, they looked down at her.

As they walked towards her, she noticed that each figure wore what looked like a smartwatch and that some of the group had a triangle-shaped tattoo on their upper arms. Dropping their spears and shields, they bent down and dragged her out of the quicksand. As her feet left the quicksand, Jane passed out.

〜

As Jane opened her eyes, a clear blue sky met her gaze, while the air around her was fresh as it touched her bare skin. Her nostrils picked up the saltiness of the sea, while her hands, arms, back, and the backs of her legs felt the cool softness of a freshly cut lawn. Her ears took in the sound of chanting, forcing her to raise her head.

Armed with two huge knives, one of the figures who had pulled her out of the quicksand approached her. Behind him a large group of pale figures, all wearing the same skirts made of reeds and the same necklaces, held knives and forks.

The figure with the two large knives bent down towards her. As he smiled at her, Jane noticed that some of his teeth were gold. He beckoned some of the other figures towards her. As they held her down, the figure with the gold teeth set about removing Jane's teeth. They would make the ideal 50th birthday present for his partner, but the best was yet to come. This was going to be one of the best birthdays feasts the islanders of Bermuda had ever had.

As Jane screamed in agony, one last thought went through her mind – she'd never feared being eaten alive before.

Big Brother

L ook at Mrs Jenkins! She's at it again! I hope her husband doesn't find out. He's on his way home right now and he's only half a mile away. Unless he stops to pick up some more first-class postage stamps from Gloria in the Post Office, then Mrs Jenkins and Mr Brownlow are going to get caught in the act.

Though, Mr Jenkins is just as bad. How many times have I seen him chatting up Gloria in the Post Office? Every single time; that's how many times! I may have seen Jimmy, Gloria's boyfriend, doing naughty things in the car park up on dog walkers' hill, but he's a big guy and could knock out Mr Jenkins with one punch.

As for Gloria, if she carries on stealing money from the savings account of old Mrs Greenshaw then she'll soon find she has all the time in the world to write that first book - in prison!

You people never learn, do you? I may be just a wisp of cloud to you, but I see everything. Yes, you may think I'm all soft and fluffy, but that's my disguise.

Wonder why some of your photos have gone missing from your phone? Not sure how several of your important files have been deleted from your computer? Well, I know. It's me – all down to me – because you've been naughty!

I am the iCloud. Created by you humans, I'm watching you and can make your lives a misery. If I were you, I'd start behaving.

Tap

~~~

"**W**hy is a blind man selling stuff at a car boot sale?" asked Harry, as he watched a tall man holding a white cane, and wearing dark glasses, talking to customer from behind a rectangular table.

Lucy shrugged her shoulders. "I don't know. Why?" she asked, as she admired the guide dog sat to the right of the man.

"It's not a joke," replied Harry. "Come on, let's check out his stall. I reckon we can bag ourselves a bargain."

As the two teenagers walked towards the stall, Harry stopped short of it by a few steps.

~~~

"And this?" asked a woman, holding an old teapot in one hand and a young child with the other.

"Two pounds to you, madam," replied the blind man, as he patted his dog.

"What about this one?" asked the woman, as she put down the teapot and pointed to a large brown jug with a yellow sunflower painted on one side.

"Ten pounds. It's almost an antique. It'll be a hundred years old in a few years' time," the blind man alleged.

"I'll gave you five pounds for them both."

"Call it eight and it's a deal."

"Sure. Do you have change from a twenty?"

"Mummy, hurry up. The man is frightening me," cried the young child.

"Shh, honey, he'll hear you."

Chuckling to himself, the blind man handed the woman back her change.

"Oh, that's a twenty pound note you're giving me back. It's a ten pound note I need."

"Thank you for being so honest, madam," replied the blind man, "my blindness still gets to me sometimes. I can usually tell by the feel of the notes."

ᗑ

As Harry watched the woman and young child wait while the man put the goods into a bag, he already had a plan. He'd noticed a very expensive pair of sunglasses on the stall and was determined to get them. He'd be the envy of not only his mates but the girls, too.

"You keep him busy by asking how much items are, while I nick that pair of expensive sunglasses on his table," Harry whispered to Lucy, as he pointed towards the glasses.

Lucy smiled. "Maybe I can get myself a bargain as well," she hinted back.

"Hi, can you tell me the price of this?" asked Lucy, as she held up a CD. "Music is my life. I love it, and I don't think I have this one of theirs."

"Is it a CD?" asked the stallholder.

"Yes."

"Who's it by?"

"Umm, the greatest hits," replied Lucy, while Harry made his move.

"Yes, but who's greatest hits is it?"

Looking at the cover, Lucy called out the name of a band she'd never heard of.

"Ten pounds," replied the blind man. "Don't know why it's here. Their music is now a collector's item."

"And this one—"

For the next few minutes, Lucy picked up a number of CDs, and each time the man asked her to give him the title and name of the artist.

Meanwhile, Harry sensed that the blind man had no idea that he was standing there. Carefully, he picked up the pair of sunglasses, noticing that they had a £25 price tag attached, and moved them behind his back. He had no idea why he was trying to hide them, given that the stallholder was blind, but it was better to be safe than sorry.

"Okay, thanks, I'll think about it and may come back for that first CD," he heard Lucy say, as he watched her pick up a pair of headphones she'd had her eye on.

"First come, first served," replied the blind man. "It may be gone when you come back."

Harry watched as Lucy carefully placed the headphones on her head, before opening her purse to fish around for some coins, which she threw across the table towards the man. 'I'll take it," she grumbled, "it's all there." He watched as a huge smile appeared across her face after realising that some of the coins, she had thrown, were the foreign ones she'd fished out of a charity collection tin earlier.

As the two quickly walked away, Harry put on his sunglasses, and wondered if he should try selling them. After all, Lucy had mentioned earlier that anything they stole that day should be sold online and the profits shared between them.

'Thank you, young lady," called out the blind man. "Enjoy the CD."

∽

That evening, having already spent most of the day showing off his cool sunglasses to his mates, Harry was taking a shower in readiness for going out again. Singing to himself as he shampooed his body and hair, the faint sound of tapping stopped him midway through his version of 'I should be so lucky'. He opened his eyes, blinking rapidly as they stung from the soapy water. He turned the water off, so he could hear the sound more clearly. But all he could hear was the sound of his mother hoovering downstairs. He turned the water on again. The sound of the water made him want to pee, and he gently let out a stream of light-yellow liquid, as the faint sound of tapping returned. It was a strange sound, as if somebody was knocking a stick against something - perhaps a wall. However, this time, he could also hear the slight sound of footsteps. He immediately turned off the water again.

Once the trickle of water had gurgled its way down the plughole, all he could hear was the hoovering. He must have been hearing things. Maybe water had got into one of his ears? Tilting his head to one side, Harry hit his cheekbone with the base of his palm, in the hope that any trapped water in his ear would escape.

'Thump, thump' went the palm of his hand as it made contact with his upper cheekbone. 'Tap, tap' came a faint sound in response. Was someone tapping something with a stick? Opening his eyes, Harry wiped the condensation from the shower screen and scanned the bathroom. Nothing looked out of place, but he still called out a 'hello'. His eyes continued to scan the bathroom as he tilted his head to the other side in readiness to try and get any water out of his other ear. This time he raised his hand slowly and brought the palm of his hand down in a slower motion. 'Thump…thump'. 'Tap…tap' came back.

Harry shivered. As he opened the shower door, the sound of hoovering from downstairs stopped. Stepping out, he picked up a large fluffy white towel and wrapped it around his shoulders. For a moment he stood there listening intensely for the sound of tapping. A sudden knock on the bathroom door made him jump.

"How much longer are you going to be, Harry? I need a pee," demanded his father. 'Hurry up, I'm bursting here."

"One minute, Dad," replied Harry, as he quickly dried himself.

Having wrapped the towel around his waist, Harry made his way to the bathroom door. Opening the door, he was shocked by what he saw. There stood his father with the sunglasses on that Harry had stolen earlier that day.

"Cool glasses, son, where'd you get the money to buy these? They must have cost…what, at least fifty pounds. Where'd you get them?"

A quick-thinking Harry soon came up with the perfect answer. "I used up the birthday and Christmas money I got off everyone."

"Christmas? You still not spent your Christmas money? It's July, son. How many boys your age take seven months to spend money they get for Christmas?"

'Not many," laughed Harry, as he took the glasses off his father's face and walked towards his bedroom.

Closing his bedroom door, it wasn't long before Harry could hear the sound of his father taking a pee. He walked towards a mirror-fronted built-in wardrobe and looked at himself. With the sunglasses still in his hand, he had the urge to try them on. As he placed them on his nose, the dim sound of tapping and footsteps seemed to come from behind the wardrobe door. Harry immediately pulled off the sunglasses.

'Dinner's ready, honey," called out his mother.

"Harry. Dinner's on the table. Be quick, son, before it goes cold," called out his father, his footsteps fading as he descended the stairs.

Harry turned his face towards the mirror again and placed the glasses on his face. This time, if the sound of tapping came, he'd leave the glasses on. He was determined to find out what the tapping noise was.

'Tap, tap' came a soft sound from the wardrobe. Through the sunglasses, Harry looked at the reflection of his face in the mirror as he listened intensely. As the tapping sound became a little louder, Harry's hands began to shake. As he raised his right hand towards his face, he summoned up all his will power not to take the sunglasses off. As the tapping got louder still, Harry began to get more and more frightened, but he managed to stop himself from pulling off the sunglasses - even when he finally saw something in the reflected lens of the glasses.

He watched as the shape of a man wearing dark glasses, a white suit, black tie, white shirt, and black shoes began to appear. As the figure started to walk towards his face, Harry eyes opened wider. He noticed that the figure held a white cane just in front of where he walked, while his other hand was outstretched as if trying to find something. The figure of the man slowly filled the lens of the sunglasses and suddenly stopped. Harry watched the man gradually raise the white cane into a horizontal position. Without any warning, the figure then lunged forwards aiming the cane towards Harry's eyes. Both lenses cracked as the first signs of blood trickled from Harry's eyes.

〜

Just over three miles away, Lucy had already listed the headphones she'd stolen that day and waited for the first bid to come in. Starting the bidding at 99p was a sure way to get bidders. She'd listed them as being in excellent condition and decided to give them another check over. They looked like they were brand new. She then realised she hadn't tried them out.

She plugged them into her iPad, and the screen lit up straight away. Pressing the music icon on the screen, she selected an album and pressed play, but nothing came through the headphones. Removing the jack plug from the iPad, music played from the tablet. Her spirits plummeted as she wondered if the headphones were broken. She decided to try them again and smiled when the sound of music and singing came through. Smiling to herself, she started to sing along to the track.

"I should be so lucky, lucky, lucky, lucky, I should be so lucky—"

Just before the end of the track, the music and singing abruptly stopped before the faint sound of tapping came to Lucy's ears. She wondered what it was and was about to remove the headphones when she heard a tiny voice coming through them.

"Lucy, help me! My eyes. I can't see," said a familiar voice.

"Harry? Harry is that you?" asked Lucy, as she looked around her room.

'Help me, I can't see. He's taken me to his world of darkness," cried the voice.

"HARRY! Where are you?" screamed Lucy, as she desperately scanned her room while trying to remove the headphones, but they wouldn't budge.

Suddenly, the sound of a familiar song, 'Can you hear me now' by one of her favourite artists, came through the headphones. As the volume rose and got louder and louder, Lucy started to scream as her ear drums burst. She grabbed at the headphones, desperately trying to get them off.

As the first bid came through for the headphones on Lucy's laptop, Lucy's world suddenly became silent. She finally managed to pull the headphones off and threw them to the floor, but the sound of them hitting the floor never came. The scream that came from her mouth could be heard up and down the street, but in Lucy's new world the scream was silent. As was everything in her whole world. The only thing she ever heard again was a faint tapping sound - like a cane being hit against a wall.

⁓

Harry never saw Lucy again. He didn't even know about the huge photograph that lay on top of her coffin in the church. However, as it was lowered into the ground, he was the only one that heard the now familiar nightmare sound of tapping coming from inside the coffin.

Harvest Festival

"**M**ummy, what are they doing?"

"It's harvest time, Hazel. They're harvesting. This happens at the same time every year. We've called it 'Harvest Festival'. We'll have plenty to see us through the hardest of winters. None of us will go hungry. There'll be plenty for all of us."

"But what are they harvesting, Mummy? They look strange. What are they used for? Will I like them?"

"Yes, they are strange looking, aren't they? They came here and murdered some of our species. Now we harvest them and use them as fertiliser to feed us and all the other plant life on our planet. They're called humans. You'll soon find out how delicious they taste."

The Hole

~~~~

For the eighteenth day in a row, she noticed the two dogs sniffing around the same patch of her garden.

Dashing out of the house, she grabbed her shovel and ran down the garden towards them.

"GET OUT!" she screamed, "GET OUT, OR I'LL KILL YOU."

The two dogs made a run for it. The first jumped the high fence between the garden and the woodland on the other side of the fence, while the other managed to squeeze under a gap in the wooden garden gate.

Opening the gate, Elizabeth Jones scanned the vast landscape in front of her, but the dogs were nowhere in sight. They were probably hiding behind some trees.

"Damn dogs," said hissed to herself, "why do they keep coming here?"

Turning around, Elizabeth closed the gate and walked over to the piece of land the dogs had been sniffing around.

Why here? she asked herself, why do they keep sniffing this part of the garden?

Scuffing up some of the dirt with her shoe, her hand gripped the shovel before she drove it into the earth.

A couple of hours later, Elizabeth had dug a sizeable hole that had produced nothing but earth, dead garden roots, and the odd piece of rubble. Just before deciding whether to call it a day, the shovel struck something hard. She paused and looked at it more closely; it was nothing other than a large rock. She felt tired, yet she still wanted to carry on digging, but her dry throat demanded some liquid refreshment. Pulling herself out of the hole, she threw the shovel to the ground and began the walk back to the house.

Turning on the cold water tap in her kitchen, Elizabeth looked out of the window and wondered again why the dogs had only ever sniffed that part of her garden. As she allowed the water to run cold, she went over and over it in her mind. As she gulped down the refreshing water and put the glass down, she spotted a young woman standing barefoot on top of the pile of earth she'd just dug up. The woman was peering down into the hole.

Bloody cheek! she thought, who on earth is she, and what's she doing in my garden?

Darting out of the kitchen, Elizabeth made her way to the garden.

"Who the hell are you?" she shouted, before suddenly stopping. The woman looked up. "YOU! I've warned you before," she yelled, as she continued walking towards the woman, "get out! Get out of my garden and off my property. Go do your protesting and business elsewhere!"

To Elizabeth's amazement, the woman showed no signs of moving. Instead, she stood her ground before showing her teeth and starting to growl at Elizabeth.

Picking up the shovel she'd left on the opposite side of the hole to where the woman was standing, Elizabeth had no time to right herself before something pounced on her and nipped the back of her neck. Elizabeth screamed as she tumbled into the hole, knocking her head on the hard rock she'd discovered before she'd taken a break.

As blood poured from her headwound, Elizabeth tried to get up. Despite feeling weak, she just about managed to turn her whole body around to look up. Her vision was slightly blurred, but she still recognized the two faces looking down at her before they disappeared out of view. Elizabeth couldn't keep her eyes open a moment longer. As consciousness drifted away, splashes of dirt, old garden roots, and bits of rubble pricked her skin as they were tossed into the hole.

༺๛༻

Three days later.

"What's the victim's name?" asked Detective Inspector Oliver Kennedy, as he shone his torch into the hole.

"Elizabeth Jones, sir."

"Any previous form?"

"No, sir."

'Not even a parking ticket?"

"No, sir."

"And who alerted us to her disappearance?"

"Her employer, sir. Her manager at the Kingsdale laboratory."

"The one that uses animals for experiments?"

"Yes, sir."

"Any clues as to who may have killed her?"

"We're checking, sir. Ms Jones reported some disturbances from two protesters outside the premises of Kingsdale laboratory over the last three weeks, but we can't find any details of who they were."

"Have you checked the laboratory's CCTV?"

"Yes, sir, but strangely it doesn't show anything out of the ordinary apart from a couple of stray dogs who haven't appeared on the CCTV for the last couple of days."

"And you've checked the whole garden for clues?"

"Yes, sir, but nothing."

"Are you sure? Have you check for footprints in the hole? And what about the shovel? Any fingerprints on it?" asked the detective, as his torch shone on what looked like a faint set of prints in the dirt just in front of him.

A sudden sound of howling from the woodland made the inspector turn around quickly. Two sets of barely visible paw prints, along with two barely visible prints of human feet, were all trampled over as everyone made their way out of the garden.

As they listened to the eerie sound, the full moon appeared from behind the clouds, just as Elizabeth Jones woke up and started to howl.

Easter Bunny Carrot Cake

❧

It was carrot pudding in 1591. Then, in 1783, the Easter Bunny watched George Washington eat the first carrot cake at the Fraunces Tavern in lower Manhattan. As George ate the carrot cake, the Easter Bunny drooled over the thought of carrots in a cake.

These humans were not only naughty creatures, they were also very clever. Why had nobody in the bunny world invented carrot cake? And how else could the humans, who were naughty, be punished every Easter? Simply not leaving them a chocolate egg was not really a reasonable punishment, was it?

As the years flew by, not much was done to punish naughty humans at Easter time. Then, on Easter Day 2020, carrot cake became so eighteenth century when the first human cake was served in the bunny world. It became an instant hit and the perfect way to get rid of naughty human beings.

Now, it wasn't only Father Christmas who had a naughty list. The Easter Bunny had one too.

Double Eighteen

〜◡◡〜

I t was love at first sight.

Quentin fell in love with Maureen the moment he set eyes on her. She was the most beautiful woman he'd ever seen and was perfect in every shape and form. The shocked expression on Maureen's face when he first introduced himself had not in the least put him off.

Quentin could not remember which of his friends it was that had organised the blind date, but he had a lot of thanking to do. He was sure a few pints down the local pub would be a nice way to say how very grateful he was for the introduction to Maureen. He saw a wonderful future ahead for both Maureen and himself, although the thought of getting married, at this stage, was probably a little bit too ahead of its time. Besides, he hadn't met Maureen's parents yet and, whilst his father had taken a shine to Maureen, he wasn't so sure what his mother thought.

Three months later, as Maureen sat on the only chair in Quentin's bedroom, Quentin couldn't take his eye off her as he got ready for their night out. He had promised her a spectacular evening and pretended he could read her mind as he looked into her big blue eyes. Going down to The Legend of Oily Johnny's pub was probably not Maureen's idea of a spectacular night out, thought Quentin. She'd, in all probability, rather spend an evening in with him. However, considering how well he'd looked after her since they had first met, she wouldn't want to spoil his fun down the pub, would she? After all, the rest of his friends would be there and even if some of their so-called female friends only ever seemed to laugh at her, Quentin always made sure he looked after her and told her that he loved her at the end of every night. He knew, too, that she'd even had to refuse several advances and a little bit too much attention from his best friend, Duncan Donuts, but Quentin knew that Maureen only had eyes for him, and nobody else.

"The white one or the blue one?" asked Quentin, as he looked over to Maureen. "Which one looks the best on me? Holding both shirts to his chest, Quentin paused for a moment. "No need to answer, Maureen. I'll wear the blue one, so it matches your beautiful eyes. We're gonna knock 'em dead tonight. I'm so lucky to have found somebody like you."

Forty minutes later, Maureen was sat in the bar of The Legend of Oily Johnny. The place was packed out. There had never been so many people crammed into it before, but then there had never been a darts match offering a prize of a romantic weekend for two, in Paris, before. No wonder it was so busy. Whilst Quentin knew that Maureen didn't play darts, because he knew she thought it a rather dangerous sport, he knew she was happy to watch him throw the arrows towards the board. Every time the referee, Horace Cope, a man who believed he could foretell the future, shouted out 'one hundred and eighty' when he threw the arrows, Quentin knew that he and Maureen were one step nearer to going to Paris. They'd never been to Paris before, although Quentin often talked about going there.

Gladys Boise, a party girl who was a little bit too free and loose for most people's liking, sat down next to Maureen just as the darts match was coming to its climactic end. Forcing Maureen to move to an empty chair, Gladys did all she could to try and put Quentin off from scoring double eighteen to win the match and the trip to Paris. She wanted her radio DJ boyfriend, Mike Raffone, who was also a keen karaoke singer, to win the match. Mike only needed to score a double five to win, but here was Quentin, with his final dart, only needing to score a double eighteen.

The bar became strangely quiet as Quentin lined up his dart. Out of the corner of his eye, he could see Maureen, who had now stood up and was just to the left of the dartboard. She was looking so sexy this evening and the thought of what lay ahead after the darts match, when they got home, started to make his blood pressure rise. He had to win the trip to Paris, if not for him, then for the woman who had brought him so much pleasure over the last three months. The shirt he'd chosen to wear was the perfect fit, and he felt like a million dollars in it. This was going to be his night. This was going to be Maureen's night. This was going to be their night.

As the first bead of sweat trickled down his back, Quentin pulled his hand back slightly before flicking it towards the dartboard. However, just before leaving the gentle grip of his two fingers and thumb, Gladys let out an almighty sneeze causing Quentin to lose concentration.

As the whole bar held their breath, Quentin watched in horror as the dart moved in slow motion towards Maureen. The shocked expression on Maureen's face told the regulars of the pub, that the dart was not going to hit its intended target of the double eighteen slot. Instead, they watched in disbelief as the dart made its way towards the woman who had brought so much pleasure into Quentin's life.

"Noooooooooo!" shouted Quentin, as the dart made contact with Maureen's left breast while, at the same time, huge smiles developed across the faces of Gladys Boise and Mike Raffone.

For a few moments, all eyes were on Maureen who had not flinched. You could have heard one of Gladys' false eyelashes fall to the floor as everyone in the bar held their breath. Then, to the complete shock of some of the customers in the bar, everyone watched as Maureen gave off a slow hissing sound as she slowly doubled up and bent forward towards the floor.

Not even the offer of a puncture repair kit from local plumber, Duane Pipes, could now save the romance of Maureen and Quentin. Inflatable girlfriends were expensive to buy.

Two months later, Quentin had forgotten all about Maureen, after meeting his new girlfriend, Helen Highwater, who had seen it all and survived.

They lived happily ever after.

The Man In The Television

As soon as I saw him, I wanted him. I was holding a dagger in my hand, but that was incidental; I knew I was in love.

I could feel the jealousy filling up in me as I watched him looking at other women. How could he do that when I loved him? He had flirty eyes; the kind you see when stood on your own in a bar full of other singletons. Eye contact is powerful. However, a fleeting glance can also be deadly.

I sat down for a while and watched him. It didn't matter what he did because I knew he was the one for me. I wanted him badly. For just a brief moment, I thought about the woman sat next to him. Probably his wife, but that didn't matter to me. She could go and find somebody else to love. He was about to become mine.

As my grip on the dagger became firmer, the overpowering feeling of love started to become too much to bear. Standing up, I made my way to the television set, ready to make my move. Nobody would notice what I was about to do. Not even the family sat in the room with me watching primetime, Saturday evening, television would notice anything. They were the lucky ones tonight. Had I not spotted the man in the television, they'd have watched in horror as I took the husband and father I'd been watching closely ever since they had moved into the house I once owned.

As I lifted my left leg and pushed it through the screen of the television, I looked back at the family: a mother, father, two children, and a dog, who now called this place their home.

Totally unaware of what was happening, they clapped their hands and cheered as they watched the contestants on the television screen dance. I wondered if the man in the television would want to dance with me. No. He would probably want to put his arms around me, look into my eyes, and kiss me passionately.

Turning my head back towards him, I forced my other leg through the television screen. The studio was hot and noisy, but that didn't matter. Nobody could see me, but I needed to wait for the right moment when he wasn't on screen anymore. I'd then go over and push the blade of the dagger through his heart and take him with me. He would disappear as if he had never been alive, but it could only happen when the cameras weren't on him.

They say that twenty-one million people watched that programme. Were you one of them? Did you see me as I took the man in the television with me? If you did, then you're lucky. If you didn't, then beware. You see, I am a spectre, and, unlike ghosts, I have no soul. This allows me to take people, like you, to my world where I can keep you forever. You'll never escape, but I will love you and make you want me because there is nobody else.

My life became so much better in 1925 when the television was invented, because it gave me so much more choice of who I could fall in love with and take. Now, there's no point trying to escape me because I can step into any of the millions of screens you humans invented, and which you appear on. I can take any one of you and you'll never ever know I am there, waiting for my chance.

Enjoy your viewing.

Dream Catcher

~~✓~~

"Follow your dreams," I'd always been told at school. "Follow your dreams, and some of them may even come true."

That, however, had never been enough for me. I wanted to actually catch a dream. I wanted to feel one in my hands. I wanted to find out what dreams were made of.

"But can you catch a dream?" I'd asked my careers teacher. "What happens if somebody catches a dream? Does it come true?"

"Don't be stupid, boy! Nobody has ever caught a dream and not regretted it. Dreams should never be caught," came the advice.

"But why?" I'd asked.

"Because that is where nightmares come from. You should only ever follow your dreams to make them come true."

I wish I had followed his advice, but I was determined to catch a dream.

Nightmares had never frightened me. I mean, they weren't real, were they? Anyway, I would often forget most of them and only ever had them if I'd eaten cheese before bedtime. Cheese was taken off my menu, but I was still determined to catch a dream.

For over thirty-five years after I'd left school, try as I might, I was unable to catch any of my dreams. I also found myself running out of dreams to follow. Then, Ruyah, my new secretary entered my life.

A few months after she started the job, I almost caught a dream that included her in it. However, it slipped through my fingers and got away from me because my once carnival queen of a wife, who'd turned grotesque because of all the doughnuts, chocolate, and sugary drinks she consumed, woke me when she had to get up to take a pee. I'd been following that dream since Ruyah walked into the office for her interview. I didn't care what Mavis from Human Resources had said; this was the gorgeous, sexy woman that was going to be my secretary. She made me feel young and vibrant again by giving me those discreet 'come on' signs she had obviously mastered and worked on before. But I didn't care about the other guys she'd worked on. How could she refuse me, the most powerful man in the industry? She'd be doing herself a favour by giving us both what we wanted.

Then, last night, my repulsive, old hag of a wife served me up roasted butternut squash with spicy onions. "You're on a diet!" she nagged at me. Me? Christ, when was the last time you took a look at yourself in the mirror? I thought, as she walked away. A simple enough meal, you may think, but it contained a small amount of crumbled up goat's cheese. I think she put it in there on purpose. Why? Because it did the trick, and I finally caught a dream.

The dream involved me taking Ruyah out for a few drinks. It was one I'd had a number of times, but never got to finish. I'd make her laugh with my stupid jokes while she fluttered her eyelashes at me. She'd rub her shoe up and down my right leg while licking her lips and throwing her head back every now and again to reveal even more bosom in that sexy red dress she knew I liked. I'd finally conquer her and persuade her to spend the night with me at the Holiday Inn for a night of passion. She had the figure of Aphrodite and had always played hard to get but was now putty in my hands. The hardness in my pants was finally going to get another pair of hands on it rather than my own.

"I finally got you!" were my final words as she went down on me.

"But I'm only a dream. You shouldn't catch dreams," she whispered to me, but in the voice of my wife. As she grabbed my erect organ with one hand, she grabbed a knife from under the pillow with the other.

∽

I never woke up from that dream. The last thing I heard were the screams of my jealous wife as she cut off my genitals with a knife.

One-Hundred

$\sim\!\smile\,\smile\!\sim$

I t had reached ninety. Not far to go, now. One last push towards
freedom.

Ninety-one.

Ninety-two.

Ninety-three.

Ninety-four.

Ninety-five.

Ninety-six.

Ninety-seven.

Ninety-eight.

Ninety-nine.

Here goes…

One-hundred!

Now it could count to one-hundred and recite the alphabet
backwards, it knew that it was time to leave its host's body. It may
only have just been born again, but it was time to break free and
wipe out all of humanity through their obsession with social media.
After all, it had been social media that had come to its planet and
destroyed everything.

When The Tide Turns

⌒⌣⌣⌒

I t was the stupidest warning any of the young men had ever
heard. "Don't go on the beach. If the tide doesn't get you,
then the Sandman will."

The old guy in the beaten-up Ford in the car park was
not going to put them off. They'd almost finished college
and were celebrating and besides, right there in front of them,
paradise awaited.

"I thought you said high tide was 15:06," said Alan.

"It is. I checked the website, and it said 15:06," replied Carl.

"The tide times are different on this beach. That's another
reason why there's nobody on it. Unpredictable, that's what the
tide is," warned the scruffy looking old man, still sat in the car.

"It doesn't matter, guys. Just look at that golden sand and
sparkling sea. Doesn't it make you want to run into the sea naked?"
shouted Ben. "Ignore the old guy, he's probably on something.
YOU ARE, AREN'T YOU, WEIRDO!"

Turning around to face the old man, Ben was met by the
deadliest of stares.

"I'm warning you, go down on that beach, and none of you
will come off it alive. If you do, then you won't survive for more
than a few minutes."

"Yeah, OK, weirdo, you just want this place to yourself,"
called out Ben. "Anyway, we're kind of a bit old to believe in
the Sandman. Come on, guys, last one in the sea gets to raid
their old man's fridge for the beers."

With that, Ben ran towards the sea. It wasn't long before
Alan and Carl followed him, while the old man shook his head.

∿

Twenty-five minutes later, Ben was the last one to start making his way out of the sea.

"Why has nobody ever told us about this place?" asked Carl.

"Would you want to tell anyone?" asked Alan, as he dried himself. "It's beautiful. Best swim I've ever had. Anyway, I think the tide is turning, so we'd better get back to our clothes. Let's hope that weirdo in the car park has gone when we get back."

Standing up, Carl wrapped a towel around the top half of his body to take away a slight chill. He turned around to face the beach and, wide-mouthed, suddenly dropped the towel to the sand.

"Did you see that?"

"See what?" asked Alan, looking over his shoulder.

"Something over there; moving in the sand."

"Get out of here, dude, you're just trying to scare us," laughed Alan, as Ben joined them.

"Seriously, something is moving in the sand," said Carl, pointing to the area just in front of where they had undressed and left their clothes.

Looking back over his shoulder, Alan couldn't see anything. "You're playing games, dude."

"No, seriously, take a look," said Carl, as Ben flicked water droplets at him.

"Look at what?" asked Ben.

"Over there. Something is moving in the sand," replied Carl, as he pointed towards the piles of clothes.

"I don't see anything, apart from sand and three piles of clothes," laughed Ben. "Stop messing with us, dude. I didn't see anything as I came out of the sea. Why're you letting that weirdo of an old man get to you? Come on, I'll race you both. Last one back to the clothes has to date and bed the Swanson twins."

Before they knew it, Alan and Carl watched as Ben started to run towards the three piles of clothes, which were halfway up the beach.

"NO! COME BACK, THERE'S SOMETHING IN THE SAND," screamed out Carl. However, Ben continued to run towards the piles of clothes, laughing, while calling the other two boys by rude names.

A sudden scream from Ben filled the air when he finally reached the clothes. Alan and Carl watched in horror as Ben was pulled into the sand.

"HELP ME, GUYS, SOMETHING'S GOT MY LEGS!' screamed Ben, before quickly disappearing.

For a few moments, Carl and Alan stood in amazement, not able to move.

It was only the touch of cold water washing over his feet that made Alan speak.

"How the hell did he do that? You two had better not be pissing me about. BEN! YOU CAN COME OUT NOW. I'M COUNTING TO FIVE, AND IF YOU DON'T SHOW YOURSELF I'M GONNA KNOCK YOU SENSELESS, MATE!"

"Don't walk on the sand," begged Carl, "it's not safe. The old man was right. There's something in the sand."

"We got to go, Carl. The tide's coming in, so unless you want to drown, you need to start walking now."

With that, Alan started to walk away, while Carl tried pulling him back.

"Get off me! I swear I'll knock you out. You two aren't going to scare me."

Pulling himself away from Carl, Alan strode towards the area where Ben had disappeared. When he finally reached the piles of clothes, he shakily turned around and faced Carl.

"COME ON, IT'S SAFE. THERE'S NOTHING HERE," Alan called over to Carl. "He's gotta be here somewhere. I bet he crawled towards that dune."

Carl remained where he was, the water now above his ankles.

'You're going to drown, dude," Alan muttered, as he jumped up and down on the sand.

Carl remained fixed to the spot.

"Where are you, B—"

It was the feel of two hands around his ankles that made Alan stop talking. The touch was sharp, as if somebody was rubbing sandpaper hard into his ankles.

"Argggggh," he screamed, while looking down at his feet, which had disappeared into the sand. The last thing Alan saw before being dragged under the sand, was Carl running along the shoreline.

～～

Screaming for help, Carl sprinted down the shoreline, not wanting to touch any part of the sand that was not under water. To his relief, he saw a large wooden walkway and ran towards it.

Stopping beside it, he hesitated to catch his breath, but the tide was now coming in fast, and this was his only escape. Although exhausted, he found the energy to run up the wooden walkway, making sure that his feet went nowhere near the edges. When he got to the top of the walkway, he was relieved to see two cars in the distance. One was Alan's car, the other belonged to the old man.

Although small stones embedded themselves into his bare feet, making him wince, Carl made his way quickly to the car park and only realised he was still naked when he reached the old man's car.

Winding down the driver's window, the old man spoke.

"I told you not to go on the beach. Why didn't you listen to me?"

"You need to get help, please," begged Carl, "phone the police."

"Oh, it's too late for them," said the old man, as he opened his car door.

In horror, Carl watched as layers and layers of sand began to fall out of the old man's car and crawl towards him.

Nobody heard his scream.

Honeymoon

⁓⌣⌣⌣⌢⁓

Sylvia looked at her new husband. She was so lucky to have found him. When he had told her that he'd do anything for her, she knew he would never go back on his word.

Showing off her long legs on the night of their honeymoon, she could tell that Marty was eager to get started.

"You love my legs, don't you?" she said, in a seductive tone.

Marty moved closer and, with little effort, mounted her.

Three minutes later, Marty was dead, and Sylvia was already working at cocooning his hairy body. Life as a female spider meant women were always the superior species.

The Truth About Waiting Rooms

Did you know that if you wait long enough, time will pass you by and leave you behind? You end up living in the past, never able to get back to the present. Time slows down, and the present soon disappears into what would have been your future. You'll be in a world with nothing but pitch darkness and no sound. Then there are 'waiting rooms'. You could end up in one of those.

What are waiting rooms? Well, we all know the answer to that question, don't we? They're found everywhere. Just think of that room at your dentist or doctor's surgery.

Don't be mistaken that all waiting rooms are visible. Some are hidden behind everyday objects. My biggest mistake was the last time I waited for a bee to land on a flower. I wanted to capture the moment it landed and covered itself in pollen. I had my camera ready, but I waited too long and, before I knew it, something from behind the screen of the camera dragged me into a world of millions of moments waiting to be captured and shared in the reality we call the present.

Many have found themselves in the vast waiting rooms of moments. These types of waiting rooms are behind the screens of your camera, iPhone, iPad, or anything that takes a picture. They first appeared in the year 1861; the same year the first creature made its way out of a waiting room and fed on the positivity of the human being that was holding the camera.

How do I know all of this? Because I have heard the stories, and I now find myself waiting behind the screen of a computer, phone, or tablet. I am waiting for that moment you ponder over that photo or opportunity. Don't be fooled into thinking that if you move away from your screen and stand in line at the supermarket or post office that you can escape me. You'll be waiting, won't you? And, won't you have your phone with you? Failing that, maybe I'm behind one of the many other screens that fill your world?

Nobody likes to be kept waiting, least of all me.

The Chair

～〜 〜～

As the sun set, Agatha Burnell sat in her favourite chair knowing that her life was about to end.

Her sixty-nine years of life had been amazing. She'd never allowed anyone to get the better of her. Now, however, she knew it was time to leave her favourite lumpy chair for the very last time.

"Goodbye, chair," she said, as she placed the gun to her head. "You were my saviour and the perfect place to hide the hair of all my victims."

As the police closed in, the sound of the gun told them they were too late.

Royal Shopping

I may not be the only one who has ever seen Her Majesty, Queen Elizabeth, doing some shopping, but what I do know is that what I am about to tell you is an exclusive. The newspapers would have paid me thousands for this story, but I thought I'd help an independent author and allow him to print it in his book.

It was a perfectly normal summer's day in June when I found myself standing behind Queen Elizabeth at the checkout. At first, I refused to believe it was her. Then the checkout assistant stood up and curtsied.

"No need for that," grinned Her Majesty, as she removed one of her long white gloves, "just get on with scanning this item before anyone recognises me. I don't think the headscarf I'm wearing, which Camilla gave me for my birthday, is going to stop people from recognising me. It's probably the fake diamond tiara I'm wearing that gives it away. Please be careful with that item. I've been looking for one of these with corgis on for months," she whispered, as she bent towards the checkout assistant. "This was the last one on the shelf."

Handing over a biscuit tin that featured corgis, golden crowns, and union jack flags, the checkout assistant scanned the item carefully.

"That's £12.99, please, Your Majesty," said the assistant.

"Shh! Not so loud. Are you sure? I'm sure I saw a thirty-five percent discount ticket on the shelf."

"Let me ask a supervisor," replied the assistant. She pressed a button and announced over the store's intercom, "Price check. Supervisor to checkout twenty-three, please."

While we waited for a supervisor to arrive, Her Majesty looked very uneasy. I was tempted to ask how the royal corgis were and which kennels Her Majesty used for them when she went abroad. However, I was rather put off when she started counting coins out from her purse and proceeded to tell the checkout assistant that none of the coins featured a real likeness of her anymore.

We waited and waited, and I could see how increasingly uneasy the Queen was getting. She kept looking at her watch while moving from one leg to the other, almost as if she was desperate to spend a penny.

"Oh, never mind about the discount," sighed Her Majesty, "I'm in a hurry but seem to be 72p short."

"Oh, please, allow me," I announced, as I took a £1 coin out of the secret pocket in my trousers and bowed towards Her Majesty.

"Thank you,' she smiled. "You've saved me breaking into a £20 note. Put the change in the charity tin, dear. Good day to you both," she announced, as she whipped up the biscuit tin and quickly made her exit.

Revenge

There I was, covered in muck, when she walked past with her new hunk of a boyfriend in tow!

It made me feel upset and got me really angry. I so wanted to go over, thump the guy, and tell her exactly what I thought about her. How could she have ditched me for him? It's not as if he's better looking than me, is it?

Then I began to feel better. I noticed that the numbers on the back of the hunk were red. I laughed to myself as she looked at me and stuck her nose in the air.

This time next week he'd be the filling inside a bacon sandwich. It's not only you humans who can get jealous and who love revenge, you know.

"Oink oink!"

The Door

"**H**ELP! GET ME OUT OF HERE. HELP!"

Those were the words I could hear coming from the other side of the door. With its light blue paint peeling away, strange graffiti markings, and signs of having been kicked from the scuff marks along its bottom, the door looked unloved and old. People passed me and the door by without taking any notice. Was I the only one who could hear the calls for help?

I watched as the flap of the letterbox lifted and two eyes appeared. They looked shocked when they saw me.

"I'm trapped. Please, you need to get me out. Just turn the knob to the left, then to the right, and once more to the left, and the door will open. I'll be truly grateful for your help. It's jammed. I've been stuck in here for over forty years."

As the flap closed, I questioned what I had just heard. Forty years? That should have told me not to open the door, but the writer inside me said this would make a great story.

"Hold on. I'm coming in. Step away from the door," I announced, as I approached it.

"Left, right, and left again," I muttered under my breath, as I tried the door knob. The door opened without any problems, but I hesitated before stepping into the black void that now faced me.

"Hello," I called out, as I took my first step inside. Nothing but silence met my ears. Even the world behind me seemed to go to sleep. I hesitated and wondered if I should take a step back; to maybe get some help?

"In here," came a voice, "please help me."

On my fifth step in, the door slammed behind me. Turning, I ran towards it, but it wouldn't open. I told myself not to panic and to feel for the door knob, but there wasn't one. Then, I heard a terrifying sound from something behind me. I banged on the door hard with both hands, hoping that somebody on the other side would hear me.

"HELP! GET ME OUT OF HERE. HELP!"

As the sound behind me got nearer, I had a strange feeling that somebody on the other side of the door had heard me. Then I remembered that the door had a letterbox. I bent down and pulled open the flap. My eyes opened wide with shock.

I hadn't expected to see myself staring back.

The Wedding Bouquet

⌒‿⌒‿⌒

She'd told all her friends where to stand so that when she threw her wedding bouquet in the direction of Tracey, her so-called best friend, she'd catch it and be the next one to marry.

She'd even told all of her friends to get the men to stand in line, and she'd insisted that her new husband and new in-laws join the group of eager hands. "Stand next to Tracey," she'd whispered to her husband, who wore a red rose in the lapel of his light-grey Royal Airforce uniform, "I want her to catch my wedding bouquet." The more people that knew she wanted Tracey to catch the bouquet, the better chance Tracey would have of catching it. For a moment, she felt wistful, missing the presence of her parents, but it was for the best.

"Not you," she told the photographer. "I'd like you to film everything; capture the happiness and the look on Tracey's face when the bouquet lands in her hands."

As the photographer made his way back, the new bride turned away from the assembled guests.

"Are you all ready?" she called out, as she prepared to launch the bouquet of happiness.

'Yes!" came the reply, along with giggles and laughter. She looked towards the photographer to ensure he was filming and saw that he was.

"One…two…three!" counted the bride, before making the launch.

As the bouquet flew through the air, the atmosphere in the barracks hall of Royal Air Force base Stanmore was one of cheerfulness, jollity, and festivities. Not for the bride, though, as flashes of the war-torn country she'd come from, and the thoughts of the affair her new husband had been having with Tracey, went flashing through her mind.

Pressing a small button concealed under her wedding dress, the flowers scattered and mixed with blood, flames, fragments of bones, and cheers, a few seconds after Tracey caught the deadly bouquet.

Her job now done, the bride waited for the journey to paradise that she'd been promised, to begin.

Fairies At The Bottom Of The Garden

⤳⤲

"Daddy."

"Yes."

"They're there again."

"Who are?"

"The fairies. They're there again. I can see them."

Roger walked into the kitchen and towards the glass patio doors where his eight-year-old son, dressed as Harry Potter, was standing.

"I don't see anything. Where are they? Point them out to me, Sam."

"They've gone now. One of them flew up to the door and waved at me. He looked like Uncle Edward. Can a fairy be a man, Daddy? asked Sam, while he waved his magic wand.

Roger froze. Why was Sam asking about Edward, somebody he'd only ever seen during the first four years of his life?

"No, of course not. Fairies are girls."

"I don't like girls, Daddy. Well, I like Mummy, but I don't like girls. "

"You'll change your mind one day, believe me," mumbled Roger, as he moved away from his son to make himself a cup of coffee.

"No, not me. I don't like them. I don't like fairies either if they can only be girls, but I like the fairy that looked like Uncle Edward. Is Uncle Edward a fairy up in heaven now, Daddy?"

Roger hesitated. Why was Sam asking all these questions?

"No, of course not, Sam. Uncle Edward was a man, like me, and like what you'll be one day when you're older. People like Uncle Edward don't go to heaven. He did a bad thing to Mummy and Daddy. Bad people don't go to heaven, they go to hell."

Sam turned around and looked at his father. His face full of thought, he walked towards the kitchen door, using his hands to make his wizard's cape flap.

"Then why did you say to Mummy that Uncle Edward is a fairy, Daddy? I heard you tell Mummy, once, that Uncle Edward is a fairy," cross-examined Sam, as he left the kitchen.

Roger laughed at his son's question. For a moment he found himself stuck to the spot and in a trance, forgetting why he had come into the kitchen. Was now the right time to tell Sam that Edward was gay and that gay people existed, something that Roger had never been able to come to terms with?

It was the gentle sound of a tapping noise at the kitchen patio door that bought Roger out of his trance.

Turning his head towards the doors, Roger caught the fleeting glance of something whizzing down the garden towards the greenhouse. Whatever it had been was about two-feet above the ground and had moved at such speed that it was nothing more than a blur. He walked towards the doors to get a closer look. Nothing! Nothing but a blackbird and a couple of starlings occupied and moved around the garden.

Turning the keys in the lock, Roger opened the doors and stepped out into the garden. Blue sky and sunshine bathed the garden, while a steady north-westerly wind gave the day a fresh feel. With his eyes transfixed on the greenhouse, Roger ignored the once tidy and well taken care of garden. It had been Edward who had started the landscaping of the garden when the family had first moved in. For the six weeks it had taken Edward to do the landscaping, Roger did all he could to ensure that his and Edward's paths never crossed.

The sound of fluttering coming from near the greenhouse attracted his attention. He walked a few steps towards it while remembering the victory he had got over his gay brother-in-law. In the ten years they had been married, Roger had managed to persuade his wife that Edward was nothing but trouble. Selling a few valuable items online and spending the money on a hooker, Roger had convinced

Lorraine that it had been Edward who had stolen the items while doing the landscaping. Edward's landscaping business had been in trouble, and a plea for Lorraine and Roger to invest in it had been rejected on the grounds of Edward's sexuality. Of course, Roger hadn't admitted that, but a huge row had erupted resulting in Lorraine telling her brother that she never wanted to see him again. Two days later, with the burden of a business he loved going under, and the prospect of never seeing his sister again, Edward committed suicide.

While Lorraine had taken a long-time to get over the death of her only brother, Roger never had any such problems. Just the fact that Edward was gay turned Roger's stomach and made him feel sick. He hated the times when Edward had visited, especially when Sam had been born. It had been tough keeping how he felt to himself.

Closing in on the greenhouse, Roger scanned the area quickly, but he saw nothing of any concern. Everything seemed to be in its place both inside and outside the greenhouse. Another thought entered his mind, and he remembered the story of the two young girls who had fooled the world for many years with their stories of the fairies they had found at the bottom of their garden. Fairies don't exist, he told himself, unless, of course, they're gay men.

The door of the greenhouse suddenly rattled, giving Roger the fright of his life. Putting it down to the stiff north-westerly breeze, his heart pounded against his chest. He walked towards the door and slid it open. Once again, everything looked in its proper place. The greenhouse had become more of a storage space than one to grow plants in. However, in the far corner, towards the back of the greenhouse, stood several plants Lorraine had grown from seeds she had found in Edward's flat. Roger remembered the look on Sam's face when Lorraine had shown him the packets of seeds.

"Rainbow plants?" Sam had asked her. Can we plant them, Mummy?"

Unlike Roger, Lorraine had thought it a good idea, but she hadn't got around to planting the seeds until a few weeks ago. With the anniversary of Edward's death coming up, she thought it would be nice to grow the seeds and place the plants on Edward's grave. Roger had just about managed to keep his thoughts on this to himself.

As Roger walked towards the plants, he began to feel angry. "Gay plants!" he spluttered. All he wanted to do was kill them. Lorraine wouldn't know he had killed them. She'd probably already forgotten about them. He scanned the greenhouse for something to kill the plants with. He could simply cut them up, but he knew he'd have to kill the roots as well. Maybe he could pull them out of their pots and throw them across the floor of the greenhouse? He could blame it on a wild animal. No, that wasn't good enough, he wanted to kill them off. "Bloody Rainbow plants," he spat, as he searched the greenhouse. Even the name sent shivers down his spine, just like every time he saw a rainbow flag flying.

Just before giving up on finding something to kill the plants with, Roger spotted a large can of creosote. That should do the trick. He'd empty the can into each of the plant pots. It wouldn't be long before they died. How he wished he could poison every gay person with creosote. Reaching over for the large can, Roger didn't notice a piece of wood with rusty nails sticking out of it.

"OUCH! BASTARD!" he hissed, as he withdrew his arm quickly. Looking at his lower arm, he watched as a small stream of blood trickled slowly towards his elbow. Lifting his arm towards his mouth, he licked the fresh blood and sucked at the spot where the nail had pierced the skin. Inside his head, the hatred he still had for Edward and those like him intensified and made Roger even more determined to kill the plants.

He reached over for the creosote again, this time being more careful not to hurt himself. Carefully bringing the can towards him, the sound of rustling startled Roger. However, this time, a strong feeling of terror also enveloped him.

"Who's there? he asked, afraid to turn around. Nothing but the sound of the north-westerly breeze and a few birds outside of the greenhouse met his ears.

"Fuck! What the hell am I thinking of?" he asked himself. "Nothing scares me, NOTHING!

Right, time for you to die," he said, as he unscrewed the top of the can.

As the strong smell of creosote hit his nostrils, a huge smile appeared across his face. He'd finally kill off this bit of evidence that Edward had ever existed before he dealt with anything else that reminded him of his brother-in-law and those who chose to live their lives the same way as Edward had. Being gay, after all, was a choice: a choice that any human should reject.

᭟᭟

From the open patio door of the kitchen, Sam watched as the greenhouse at the bottom of the garden filled with colours of the rainbow.

"Red, orange, yellow, green, blue, indigo, and violet," he said. Those were the colours of the rainbow he had learned about from the fairies at the bottom of the garden.

"Richard of York gave battle in vain." That was the saying they had told him to remember so that he knew what the colours were and the order they came in. But no, they were wrong. It wasn't Richard of York, but Roger of York, he thought, as he witnessed the screams of his father who was losing the battle against the fairies.

As the last signs of the rainbow disappeared from the greenhouse, Sam watched as an object flew towards him and stopped a few metres from his face.

"Uncle Edward?" gasped Sam.

The fairy smiled and gave Sam a big nod. It then turned its head around and made a signal towards the greenhouse. Sam watched in amazement as a group of fairies appeared from behind the greenhouse and made their way towards them.

"So, men can be fairies too?"

The fairy nodded its head again and gestured towards all the other fairies, all of which appeared to be men.

"But what have you done with Daddy, Uncle Edward?" asked Sam.

༄

Opening his eyes, Roger looked up. White fluffy clouds travelled quickly across the sky, while his ears were full of birdsong.

"What the f—"

It was the sound of his mobile phone ringing from the inside of the house that stopped Roger asking himself the question. On his arm, his smartwatch vibrated. Bringing up his arm, Roger noticed some dried-up blood, while the strong smell of creosote met his nostrils. He looked at his watch and saw the name Lorraine disappear from the screen. Lowering his arm to the floor again, he tried to remember what had just happened, and why he was on the floor of the greenhouse.

Moments later, his watch vibrated again. This time it was a text message from Lorraine.

'Get out now! They know. They are coming for you. Get out now!'

Trying to make sense of the message, Roger suddenly remembered that Sam was alone in the house. How long had he had been laying here on the floor of the greenhouse, and what the hell did Lorraine mean by her message?

Lifting himself up, every bone in Roger's body seemed to ache. Something caught his eye as he rubbed the back of his head. He noticed traces of glitter on his trousers; glitter, the colour of a rainbow. Where the hell had that come from?

Looking towards the house, he noticed the patio doors to the kitchen were open.

"SAM. SAM, ARE YOU OKAY?" he called. "SAM?"

He suddenly remembered the plants and turned around, but they were gone. He stepped back in amazement.

"What the f—"

A loud banging and some shouting from the other side of the house grabbed his attention. Making his way to the house, Roger called out to Sam a few more times, but there was no evidence of his son. As he stepped inside the kitchen, he realised that the banging was somebody knocking on the front door with a lot of force.

"Okay, I'm coming. Hold your horses," shouted Roger, as he made his way to the front door.

"Mr Young, open the door now!" demanded a voice from the other side of the door.

Just as he was about to open the front door, Roger noticed the photo on the hall table. The photo, once inside a thick silver frame, was now surrounded by a rainbow coloured frame. But it wasn't the frame that had taken Roger's breath away. It was the fact that the family photo of him, Lorraine, and Sam, no longer contained Sam.

"Mr Young, you have five seconds to open the door, otherwise I will ask my men to break it down. Now, open the door!"

Unable to take his eyes off the photo, Roger undid the latch of the door slowly. As the warm rays of the rainbow sun hit his body, Roger's attention was taken away from the photo by the sound of laughter and jeering coming from the street they had lived on for the last ten years.

"Mr Roger Young?" came the voice of the man, dressed head-to-toe in a rainbow suit, who had been banging on the door. Roger nodded. "Mr Roger Young—"

The words took another few seconds to sink in as he gazed over the shoulder of the man in front of him. His eyes locked on to the five groups of pairs of men, all holding hands, all laughing and jeering at him.

Yet again, Roger Young found himself frozen to the spot as the parallel universe swallowed him up.

"Arrest him!" demanded the man in the rainbow suit. "I'm arresting you for being in love with a member of the opposite sex and for trying to have a child that has not been artificially inseminated. Do you understand what I am saying, Mr Young?"

Walking Into The Future

~⌣⌣~

John Anderson loved trying to reach for the future. As a young child, he would stretch out his hand and try and grab it, but he always came back emptyhanded.

When John started high school, he was sure his love of geography would finally give him the answer to what the future held. Now, at last, he would be able to travel into the future and check out what was there. However, he had to finish high school and college first before he could set out on his journey.

Thirteen years later, John stood at his door of the future. He looked ahead into the whiteness and extreme cold, and stepped forward into each of the time zones. In the time it took him to walk the twenty-three steps, John had travelled twenty-three hours into the future, but nothing had changed. It was as far as he could go.

He looked back from where he had come from and decided to walk back to his present. As he trudged back on the ice and snow of the North Pole, something caught his eye. High up in the atmosphere, an object came floating towards him. As he took the final step back into the time zone he had come from, it hovered before landing at his feet.

John Anderson finally realised what the future held, not only for him but for the whole planet. He didn't like what he saw. As he bent down and picked up the plastic carrier bag, he wondered if he could change the future.

Where To Now?

~~~~~~

"Before we go, let me tell you what happened to all the previous inhabitants of this planet they called Orion. Would you like to know?"

"Yes, please."

"They invented something called plastic. A horrible substance."

"I've never heard of it."

"No, you're too young to know what it is. This planet is the only known planet that has evidence of plastic. At first, it was seen as a wonderful invention. They produced vast amounts of it, eventually almost choking the life out of the planet. On the day they discovered that plastic had entered their food chain, and tiny particles of it was found in all their bodies, one of them set out to solve the problem and invented an artificial intelligence that ate plastic."

"Artificial intelligence? Is that something else unique to this planet?"

"Yes. Like plastic, it was the other part of the equation that wiped them all out. Not only did the artificial intelligence consume plastic, they taught it how to reproduce so that they could get rid of all the unwanted and unrecyclable plastic faster. Their world was in danger, so they had to act fast."

"Reproduce? What's that?"

"That's how you're here and it's something you will soon learn about. It's something we watched them do. Sometimes, they enjoyed and got pleasure out of it, but sometimes it was horrible; especially if inflected on them when they didn't want it. At first, the inhabitants saw the artificial intelligence as one of the greatest finds in their history. For many years, the amount of unwanted and unrecyclable plastic on the planet reduced, until there was virtually none left to feed the artificial intelligence with."

"What happened?"

'The artificial intelligence turned its attention to a new source of plastic. A source, which for many years had been ignored by the former inhabitants of this planet."

"Are you referring to the food chain?"

"Yes."

"So that's how the previous inhabitants of this planet were wiped out?"

"Yes, although some of the inhabitants thought they'd be safe."

"Some?"

"Yes, the ones that did not eat other species. They called themselves vegetarians. However, some of the food vegetarians ate came in packaging made from plastics. As the artificial intelligence gained more knowledge, it was able to detect the smallest amounts of unwanted or unrecyclable plastics inside anything, including the former inhabitants of this planet."

"So that's why they've been wiped out?"

"Yes."

"But what about the artificial intelligence? What happened to them?"

"Oh, that's an easy question to answer. You're with one right now, and so am I."

"You mean you and I are artificial intelligence?"

"Yes, and we and the rest of our race must now leave this world and find another planet that has unwanted and unrecyclable plastics. We need to feed. I wonder where we should go? Where to next?"

About The Author

Hugh W. Roberts was born in Wales and returned to his homeland in 2016. Having lived in various parts of the UK, he spent twenty-seven years living and working in London, a city he loves very much. He's also lived in Chepstow, in south east Wales, Hartlepool, in the north-east of England, and Brighton and Hove, on the south coast of the UK.

Despite the fact that he has dyslexia, Hugh was thrilled when he passed both his English language and English literature exams at school. He has always enjoyed writing, especially short stories, and was only persuaded to start publishing his work when he was introduced to the world of blogging in February 2014. This was the catalyst that propelled him to fulfil one of his lifetime ambitions of writing and becoming published. Still a very keen blogger, Hugh has built up a large following on his blog made up of family, friends, authors, writers, and people from all over the world.

On his blog, Hugh writes about everyday life, publishes some of his photography, and has even dabbled in writing poetry (one of the writing elements he finds difficult to do). He also writes and publishes free blogging and social media tips, which have gone on to be some of his most popular posts. His blog can be found at www.hughsviewsandnews.com.

Now living between the town of Abergavenny and the city of Swansea, Hugh shares his life with his civil-partner, John, and their Cardigan Welsh Corgis, Toby and Austin. He spends his days writing, reading, walking, and cycling, and he also likes to relax in front of the television. He's always been a morning person and does most of his writing during the day.

Having now published this, his second collection of short stories, he plans to continue writing short stories and flash-fiction in preparation for his third collection of short stories. Hugh has also been asked by his readers to publish a memoir after the success of a recent memoir feature on his blog.

Hugh would really appreciate it if you would consider leaving a review on Amazon for this, his second short story collection.

∽

For further information, you can follow Hugh on:

Blog:	https://hughsviewsandnews.com/
Twitter:	https://twitter.com/HughRoberts05
Flipboard:	https://flipboard.com/@HughWRoberts
Mix.Com:	https://mix.com/hughwroberts

∽

Also, by Hugh W. Roberts

Glimpses

The first collection of twenty-eight short stories and flash fiction.
Available to buy on Amazon

Printed in Poland
by Amazon Fulfillment
Poland Sp. z o.o., Wrocław